PRAISE FOR
T

"Libby McNamee has created another exciting historical fiction novel for middle grade readers! From First Lady Dolley Madison's perspective, the reader will feel like a fly on the wall listening to intimate conversations about the political and social events happening during the War of 1812. Rich with historical details and imagery, this novel introduces young readers to an important time period with a strong and resilient main character. Loved this up close and personal account of history and can't wait to share it with others. Huzzah!'

—Donna Wilson, Librarian, Robious Middle School, Midlothian, Virginia

"McNamee has written another exciting novel— replete with historical details and a lively portrayal of a smart, determined woman who is devoted to her husband and country. From the first sentence, we are breathlessly pulled into Dolley Madison's fascinating journey as First Lady and root for her every step of the way as she navigates politics and power during a turbulent period in American history."

—Kathryn Goodwin Tone, award-winning author of *The King's Broad Arrow*

"Libby McNamee firmly places Dolley Madison where she belongs—as the first lady at the epicenter of the War of 1812 and as the protagonist in her own story. McNamee graciously introduces young readers to a heroine and a female founder too often overlooked for having both made and saved American history."

—Karen A. Chase, award-winning author of *Carrying Independence*

"Libby Carty McNamee has done it again! She excels at bringing real women from history to life for middle grade readers. Her new novel about Dolley Madison is full of rich historical details and important events from this little-known time period, all told in a propulsive story that is exciting for children. Your child will feel like they are fleeing the British alongside Dolley! Huzzah!"

—Jayda Justus, founder of *The History Mom*

"McNamee has a real talent for putting the reader in a relatable front-row seat to exciting events of the past. Dolley Madison is a force to be reckoned with in this fascinating tale of the influential First Lady in a lesser known period of American history."

—Steven K. Smith, author of *The Virginia Mysteries*

"McNamee's mastery with the pen creates characters with depth that intrinsically tie in historical accuracy to play out in a way that exhibits a paragon of historically-themed literature. Dolley's story is our national hiSTORY, and it engages students of all ages to let the words take them back in time."

—Judith Kalaora, Artistic Director, *History At Play,* and Portrayer of Dolley Madison

"Readers young and old will enjoy traveling back in time to witness the first time our democracy was threatened by a foreign foe. Libby McNamee offers this story not from a military perspective but from that of Dolley Madison, the First Lady. McNamee shares the story as if she overheard the conversations herself, and she enables her readers to be there, too. A great read for all ages."

—Annette Benbow, Director of the Historic Ball-Sellers House, Arlington, Virginia

"Libby McNamee once again brings a period of American history to life. In *Dolley Madison and the War of 1812*, she drops her readers into the center of James 'Jemmy' Madison's inauguration, depicting 'Washington City' when Pennsylvania Avenue was the only real thoroughfare. The story of how the United States struggled in the Second War of Independence as told by the narrator, Dolley Madison, reveals the true loyalty, dedication, and patriotism of her husband, the 'Father of the Constitution.' Dolley's role in supporting her husband, establishing American traditions, and forging amicable relationships between Republicans and Federalists by opening the presidential home to the masses was invaluable. She gave birth to the national spirit that contemporary readers know today!

McNamee has an amazing ability to weave enormous amounts of fascinating historical information while engaging the reader with the contributions and relationships between important figures such as Thomas Jefferson, Henry Clay, James Monroe, Congressman Randolph, John C. Calhoun, Andrew Jackson . . . the list goes on. Her details and dialogue allow us to view them as real people with strengths and weaknesses, successes and failures.

Readers cheer for the irrepressible Dolley

Madison's and her bravery to save George Washington's portrait and Abigail Adam's clock during Cockburn's siege on the city, and they marvel at her ability to rise above those who criticized and found fault in her beloved husband. She emerges as a true American heroine. McNamee illuminates Dolley Madison's contributions to the United States in this fascinating novel so that she will not be forgotten. Whether you are interested in reading about details of battles, contributions of Madison's slaves, or what Dolley served (or wore!) to her 'squeezes' or State Dinners, this book has something for every reader.

As an English teacher, Libby McNamee's first novel, *Susanna's Midnight Ride*, provided an excellent companion read and subject for rigorous literature circles with my sixth-grade students when they studied the Revolutionary War in social studies class. *Dolley Madison and the War of 1812* will be another novel to bring history alive for students. And for that, I say, *'Huzzah!'*"

—Joanne Stanley, 6th and 7th Grade English Teacher, Center-Based Gifted Program, Swift Creek Middle School, Midlothian, Virginia

"A heart-pounding, front-row seat to young America's fight for survival through the eyes of the Queen of Hearts: First Lady Dolley Madison. Walk arm and arm with Dolley to experience the tentative beginnings of her beloved 'Jemmy' Madison's Presidency as she wields her secret weapon of charm to win the respect, honor, and love for her husband and 'the people's house.'

Empathize with her as her initial joy of

transforming the deplorable President's House into a respectable, inviting home filled with guests and new traditions is replaced with horror when the British burn it to the ground, along with all of Washington City in the War of 1812.

Marvel at her fierce determination to stand by her man and her country with mud in her shoes and verbal mud on her face hurled by opposing voices.

Cheer as Dolley grabs America by the hand to lift her up from the dark mire of war to stand as a tall beacon of light for the world as they triumphantly sing the newly penned 'Star-Spangled Banner.'

Libby McNamee brings this dark moment of American history to life through an intimate telling rich with historical facts, vivid imagery, and thrilling action. 'Hail to the Presidentess' and her talented scribe!"

—Jenny L. Cote, award-winning author of *The Amazing Tales of Max and Liz* and *Epic Order of the Seven* series

DOLLEY MADISON AND THE WAR
OF 1812

DOLLEY MADISON AND
THE WAR OF 1812

America's First Lady

LIBBY CARTY MCNAMEE

Hail to the Presidentess,
Queen Dolley!
Libby McNamee

ALSO BY LIBBY CARTY MCNAMEE

Susanna's Midnight Ride: The Girl Who Won the Revolutionary War

Study Guide for Susanna's Midnight Ride: The Girl Who Won the Revolutionary War

Study Guide for Dolley Madison and the War of 1812: America's First Lady

For more information, please contact:

Sagebrush Publishing

Richmond, VA

www.SagebrushPublishing.com

Libby@SagebrushPuublishing.com

ISBN: 978-1-7322202-4-9

❀ Created with Vellum

For Bernie, My Jemmy

"I was beaten by Mr. and Mrs. Madison. I might have had a better chance had I faced Mr. Madison alone."

— CHARLES PINCKNEY, JAMES MADISON'S
PRESIDENTIAL OPPONENT IN 1808

CONTENTS

PROLOGUE
AUGUST 24, 1814

The danger that threatens me right now is worse than any nightmare because it is real. The same British warriors who brought down Emperor Napoleon of France are marching into Washington City at this very moment. They plan to burn it, take me prisoner, and then parade me through the streets of London. What a disgrace for America to witness Dolley Madison, the wife of its fourth president, carried off in chains.

To my horror, I am one of the last residents left in this tiny town; everyone else fled hours ago. Even the hundred soldiers that my dear husband ordered to guard the President's House with their lives melted away into the massive exodus. As for me, I've refused the mayor's desperate pleas to head for safety in Virginia. Of course, I couldn't leave without President Madison. For hours I've packed trunk after trunk with his official papers, awaiting his return from the battlefield in Bladensburg where our panicked troops sprinted away from the mighty British invaders.

Alas, I cannot wait any longer. The boom of the cannons rattles the windows of the President's House, and the sulfuric

I

odor of gunpowder hangs heavy in the air. The British forces are closing in. I must flee now or I am doomed to become their captive. There are so many cherished belongings in our home that I would love to save, but I have neither the time nor the room.

I need to leave this second, but I race into the dining room to grab some last pieces of silver. There I stop with a gasp, finding myself face-to-face with the life-sized portrait of General Washington.

"Take down this painting. I won't leave without it!" I shout to my servants. After hosting enormous receptions here for years, it's hard to believe that I now stand alone, the only one left to save the Father of Our Country.

CHAPTER 1
ONWARD TO THE CAPITOL
MARCH 4, 1809

My heart soars as I take in the thousands of fellow Americans lining muddy Pennsylvania Avenue while we make our way to today's momentous event. While some cheer us on, others jeer us. How I wish for the time to stop and meet everyone, even our hecklers. Alas, this primitive road looks more like the lane to a pig farm than an elegant roadway leading to our unfinished Capitol.

Thud! Our green carriage emblazoned with silver M's lurches to an abrupt halt. The cavalry troops stand by in their full regalia, waiting to escort us again. We teeter at a precarious angle, stuck in a deep rut.

Gritting his teeth, our young coachman Paul does his best to navigate the four straining horses out of it. He's such a handsome boy and so smart, too.

"I can't believe this is happening," mutters my husband, James Madison.

I rest my hand on his arm and smile, confident we won't be late. After all, I'd carry him on my back if necessary. I'm four inches taller and outweigh him by more than I care to admit. Plus, I am seventeen years younger.

3

However, poor Paul looks over his shoulder at us, his face drawn. "Don't worry, Mr. Madison. We'll be fine in just a minute. I promise." Despite his age, he is quite reliable. Among other responsibilities, he shaves my husband's face every morning and freshens his black coat, breeches and silk stockings.

"This brief delay doesn't concern me at all, Paul." He looks off into the crowd. "It's the new post that I'm taking on today."

"You'll do a brilliant job, Jemmy." I pat his knee. "You helped found this country, and you'll make a marvelous leader, too."

"My dear, it's not just the position, but the current crisis that grieves me." He rubs the back of his neck. "Why should it be any different for me than President Jefferson? Even as his Secretary of State for eight years, we couldn't make the British see reason. And our trade embargo against them was an utter disaster, only hurting ourselves."

I glance over at him and then study his face. "Jemmy, did you sleep at all last night?" The purple bruises underneath his eyes worry me.

He shrugs, but I know the answer is no. When I awoke this morning, he was in the same position as when I fell asleep—propped against his pillow, still mulling over his speech. The only change was his candle which had burned down to the wick overnight.

"What really worries me is forming my Cabinet. The options are dismal. Of course, Gallatin is brilliant as Secretary of the Treasury, but the others are pathetic. They're either a friendly enemy, a political necessity or a drunk." He shakes his head. "And some are all three. But the worst part is they all despise each other."

"You'll make the best of it. We have no choice." As the

carriage finally rolls forward onto even road, I give his hand a squeeze.

"No, we certainly don't." Jemmy's tone is glum. "But I feel like I'm headed to the guillotine. No wonder our outgoing president wouldn't come with us and insisted on riding horseback alone. President Jefferson doesn't want to risk getting accidentally sworn in again. I wouldn't either."

I turn to look him in the eye. "Remember, you won this election by a wide margin. The American people have great faith in you, and so do I."

As usual, my thoughts turn to my son at boarding school in Baltimore. "I'm disappointed Payne can't attend the ceremony today, but I understand. He's so busy with his studies." It's a shame his grades are poor, but he claims to work hard. His effort is what really matters. And all those rumors about his drinking escapades are quite unfair. I can't help myself from doting on the poor boy. He lost so much when just a tot —both his father, John Todd, and his baby brother, William, to ghastly yellow fever. The massive epidemic devastated Philadelphia, taking ten percent of the population, and my in-laws as well.

Much to my delight, though, little Payne hung on Jemmy's suit during their first meeting. His kind nature also drew me in right away. Soon he became my darling, dearest, and best friend. We married within three months of our acquaintance on his parents' anniversary. What a joy to give my hand to the man I so admired. Even after fifteen years together, we still detest spending any time apart. Let others say he is sour and forbidding all they want. I do my best to not let them upset me, but choose to pity them instead. With his sparkling blue eyes and generous soul, Jemmy is the greatest blessing of my life.

"I agree, my dear. I'm sure he's doing his best. He's smart to focus on his academics. Perhaps he will get into Princeton after all and follow in my footsteps." As Payne's adoptive father, Jemmy indulges me by indulging him. Alas, neither of us can refuse him anything. "We'll hear from him soon enough, once he needs more money." I laugh, knowing how accurate that is.

Soon we arrive at our nation's most important building, amazed by the additional 10,000 citizens who await us there. We fall into silence, listening to the dramatic clamoring of our countrymen who stand outside the carriage. Ah, the free spirit of America is alive as the people shout their conflicting opinions. As the author of the Bill of Rights, Jemmy helped guarantee this exercise of free speech.

"Hail to the Queen Elect. Huzzah!" calls out a lady in a shrill voice.

"Go back to Virginia, little Madison, and take that fool Jefferson with you!" growls an angry old man.

"Mrs. Madison, I love your new turban!" gushes a sweet woman.

"Let's stand up to those British bullies. Our national pride is at stake!" bellows a gentleman in back.

"Don't take us to war. We're not prepared! You'll be the ruin of this country," shouts a young man.

"We'll never be their obedient Colonists again!" shrieks a defiant old woman.

"God bless you, Mr. and Mrs. Madison!" cries a young girl.

"You only won by a landslide because of her!" booms a deep voice.

Jemmy nudges me, his eyes merry. "That last shout, my dear, is the absolute truth."

CHAPTER 2

THE HALL OF REPRESENTATIVES

Now I stand in the exquisite Hall of Representatives alongside Thomas Jefferson, our third president. However, on this historic day, an enormous crowd gathers in their finest apparel for the inauguration of our next president, James Madison. This oblong octagon is our country's largest and most sophisticated room with a soaring wooden dome and one hundred crystal skylights. We take great pride in it, believing it even more splendid than Great Britain's House of Commons.

Much to my delight, everyone gawks at me, craning their necks for a glimpse of my elaborate outfit. Needless to say, I adore the limelight just as much as Jemmy flinches from it. We're opposites in many ways, but our hearts understand each other.

My heart goes out to Jemmy waiting at the podium. Although quite prestigious, serving as our nation's president is a thankless job, especially right now. He will soon preside over this divided country. We Republicans find ourselves bitterly at odds with the Federalist Party formed by

Alexander Hamilton. Unfortunately he perished five years ago in a duel against our former friend, Aaron Burr.

"Poor Jemmy's lost all color. He's like a ghost with ruby red lips," I mutter to Mr. Jefferson. Of course, Jemmy is pale by nature, but this is concerning.

Leaning down, he whispers in my ear, "I am much happier at this moment than my friend." His fringed blue jacket from France has large metal buttons, which set off his red hair and red velvet waistcoat. Although our incoming and outgoing presidents could not look more different, they are close political allies and the best of friends.

"Indeed, I've never seen him so nervous." Then I seize the opportunity to rib Mr. Jefferson. "Well, you're the one who got us into this fine mess, convincing my husband to join your Cabinet eight years ago." I wave my arm. "There we were, enjoying life at Montpelier with glorious views of the Blue Ridge Mountains when you brought us to this primitive town."

"It's no secret that Mr. Madison will inherit a colossal mess from me." Mr. Jefferson shakes his head as if trying to make all the problems go away. "I dare say it will become a second fight for our independence from Britain."

"Yes, I dread another conflict with them, but it's inevitable." I smooth the pleats in my skirt. "For now, though, we must celebrate—or at least pretend we are."

"No one will enjoy today more than me." Mr. Jefferson cracks a wry smile as I give him a playful elbow to the ribs.

As the Sergeant at Arms calls the boisterous crown to order, Mr. Jefferson turns to move elsewhere, so I grab his arm. "Don't be silly. There's a seat for you right here in the front row."

"This day I return to the people, and my proper place is among them." Mr. Jefferson shakes his head and makes his way to the back, thrilled to become a private citizen once again. Even with his slouch, he still stands tall above the crowd with his lanky build and broad shoulders. He's earned the nickname Long Tom for his six-foot-two stature.

I take my seat, nestling in between my dear sisters so we can launch into some light-hearted banter. Our bond is so tight that people often refer to us as the Merry Wives of Windsor after the Shakespearean comedy.

"I'm so thankful for the sun," announces Anna, my youngest sister who is more like my daughter. "It sets an optimistic tone on such an important day." She is married to Congressman Richard Cutts of Massachusetts. They have three wonderful boys, the oldest named for Jemmy, as well as a darling daughter, Dolley, after me. I love my nephews and niece just as dearly as my own precious Payne.

"I'm just grateful the roof isn't leaking onto my new gown," I muse, running my fingers along its fine fabric. "That brown water would stain this cambric and make Sukey quite cross. After all, she'd have the impossible job of cleaning it."

"And this spring temperature is perfect, too," adds Anna. "There isn't an inch to spare in here, but at least we aren't roasting like during the summer." She fans herself with her hand. "Just thinking about it makes me hot."

"Yes, this is much more pleasant. I much prefer eating oysters in my iced creams rather than feeling like a baked oyster myself."

Anna laughs as I fluff my skirt and chatter. "I don't usually wear white, but I think it adds a lovely layer of formality for this important State occasion. After our Quaker upbringing, I certainly do enjoy the evil temptations of the material world." I sigh. "How I adore French fashion, even if I can't speak a word of the language."

"Do you like it, Lucy?" I ask, glancing over at my other younger sister. As usual, her silence worries me. It is so unlike her normal bubbly temperament.

Her lower lip trembles, and my heart sinks. I can't bear to see her cry again, not after her tears this morning. Years ago, she eloped with General Washington's favorite nephew, George Steptoe Washington. To her overwhelming sadness, her husband recently died of consumption, and she became a grieving widow with three boisterous sons to raise alone. They live with us, and we help as much as we can.

"What do you think of this?" I put a hand to my extravagant matching turban. "After all, good Quaker women are supposed to cover their heads."

Lucy musters a wan smile as she gazes down at her husband's pocket watch. Nowadays the poor dear refuses to go anywhere without it.

I prattle on, trying to distract her. "Of course, it's not Quakerly at all. But I must say, the glossy sheen of the silk is quite eye-catching."

Anna points to my white ostrich feathers with a cackle. "They look like giant punctuation marks jutting into the air!"

With my nerves on edge, I ramble. "Some people may call me frivolous, but dressing well shows confidence and pride, something we need more of here in America."

"Are you sure that's not just an excuse to order more gowns from Paris?" Anna teases me with a smirk.

I play along, giving her a fierce look of mock indignation. "We do have our troubles, but the future is bright. When Jemmy negotiated the Louisiana Purchase for President Jefferson six years ago, he doubled our size and opened up an amazing amount of land on our western frontier. Now we're up to seventeen states with Louisiana coming soon! And let's not forget our population has doubled, too. But the best part is controlling the Mississippi. That river is our best resource. After all, traveling by water is so much easier than the road. It's hard to believe it runs all the way down to New Orleans and the Gulf of Mexico."

Anna puts a hand to her brow and announces, "I've heard this speech so many times I can repeat it myself." With an impish grin, she recites, "'We do have our troubles, but the future is bright.'"

"Well, I'm glad you've been paying attention." I fold my arms and pretend to get into a huff.

Glancing over at the podium, I lock eyes with Jemmy, and my heart swells for his unwavering patriotism. How I want him to succeed. My husband's greatest love, other than me, is our country. He has dedicated his life to bringing the lofty ideal of liberty into reality, starting as a young man who risked his neck by rebelling against King George III.

"Jemmy appears quite dapper," Anna whispers, admiring his new American-made black suit and top hat. Like a traditional revolutionary, he wears knee breeches with stockings and ties his powdered white hair back in a bow. George Clinton, Mr. Jefferson's Vice President, sits to his left. He will soon become Jemmy's Vice President as well. Chief Justice John Marshall is on his right, wearing the flowing black robe of the Supreme Court.

My heart races as Jemmy breaks out in a sudden sweat and sways from side to side.

"Oh dear, he looks like he's about to faint." Lucy whispers a moment later. She's back on the verge of tears again.

"He certainly does." I fan myself with my French lace handkerchief, wishing I could cool him off instead.

"Now his hands are shaking." Anna whispers as Jemmy pulls out his notes. "I hope he can read his speech." He stands so high on his tiptoes that even his silver buckles face forward. Alas, he fools no one. He is by far the smallest man in this cavernous room. However, I remain steadfast. After all, his brilliant mind towers over everyone.

"Is Little Jemmy really ready to be president?" scoffs

Congressman Daniel Webster of New Hampshire, seated behind me. I pretend not to hear.

Then another snide remark invades my ears. "America is doomed for too many reasons to list." Without even looking, I can identify the high pitch and ugly tone of Congressman John Randolph of Virginia. Unfortunately, he is Mr. Jefferson's cousin, one whom he would love to disown.

I am seething on the inside. The inauguration has yet to begin, yet already they criticize him. These ungrateful people deserve a tongue-lashing. Instead, I bat my eyes and hold my tongue. This is nothing new unfortunately. The Federalists call him many names that I refuse to let pass my lips. However, as the Father of the Constitution and architect of the Bill of Rights, he is a firm believer in every American's right to insult him.

"But Randolph is doomed to be himself!" Lucy whispers in my ear. She lets loose a clownish hoot, so rare these days. I should scold her, but I'm too busy savoring her happier mood and holding back a snicker myself.

"They're just jealous!" grumbles Anna under her breath.

Jemmy refused to campaign because he considered it bad manners. So, I took matters into my own hands and rallied the votes on his behalf. Nonetheless the contest was ugly and full of lies about so many things, even the state of our marriage. I can ask God to help me forgive these despicable attacks, but they won't stop now. If anything, they will worsen. After all, John Adams, our second president, was mocked as "His Rotundity" throughout his term.

I do my best to distract my darling husband from his worries, but he has far too many. If I could have my way, I'd never leave his side. I'm most content when standing in the shadow of his great intellect.

As Jemmy launches into his inaugural address, I have no doubt his first words as our president are profound. However,

I can't hear a thing, even sitting so close. I wring my hands, hidden underneath my handkerchief.

Turning my head a few inches, my dear friend Hannah Gallatin and I exchange raised eyebrows. Her husband Albert is the Secretary of the Treasury. Next to her, Margaret Bayard Smith of Washington City's only newspaper, the *National Intelligencer*, sneaks me an encouraging wink. We are so fortunate to have the press on our side, an invaluable ally. Public speaking isn't important for a successful presidency, I reassure myself. It only gives the Federalists another opportunity to criticize Jemmy. President Jefferson avoided it altogether, only giving his two inaugural addresses. He even mailed his State of the Union Address to Congress every year rather than delivering the speech in person.

Much to my relief, Jemmy gains momentum as he plods along, outlining his goals to remain neutral in the European war between France and Great Britain, foster a spirit of independence, and respect the rights of individual states. I am elated when he declares, finally at full volume, "It has been the true glory of the United States to cultivate peace by observing justice." Then his voice cracks.

"Heaven, help us," I whisper, grabbing my sisters' hands. I pray no one noticed and give a vigorous nod of approval, knowing my bobbing feathers are on full display. Even though I don't feel confident, I must act as if I am.

Jemmy is now the leader of the Republicans, the party that he and Mr. Jefferson created together. Now the weight of our young democracy rests upon his frail shoulders. I'm so proud of him and my country, yet so scared for them both, too. He is at the center of a brewing political storm, facing the impossible task of pleasing everyone despite their opposing views.

As we witnessed with President Jefferson, the burden of this office is crushing. Our nation suffers from a nasty divide between the Republicans and Federalists. Alas, their mutual loathing is no secret. With such deep animosity, we hardly seem like one people. However, our European foes do give us a common enemy that helps to unite us. Without that bond, our differences would tear us apart.

After more than fifteen years, the French and British Empires remain mired in war. Let there be no mistake; both rulers are contemptuous. The ruthless Emperor Napoleon battles Britain's King George III who went mad after losing the War of Independence to us, their former rebellious Colonists. Much to our frustration, the British and the French insist on entangling us in their current hostilities, ignoring our repeated pleas to stay uninvolved. We have become the pawn of both countries as they try to prevent us from trading with the other.

Great Britain is the worse of the two by far, abusing us like a nasty older brother. For years now, they've had the gall to snatch thousands of American sailors from our ships and force them to serve in their Royal Navy. To make matters worse, their settlers in Canada encourage the Indians on our new western frontier to rebel against us and even provide them with weapons to do so. Shame on them! It's high time to defend our honor. Unfortunately, we must use force to show them in no uncertain terms that we are no longer their subjects. Furthermore, we will never become subservient to them again.

Despite the stuffy heat, my dark thoughts make me shiver. Recalling my formal surroundings, I square my shoulders. Tucking my wayward black curls under my ornate turban, I paste on a triumphant smile and clasp my hands together. My stomach is as turbulent as the Atlantic where the British kidnap our men, but I can't let on. No one must know.

CHAPTER 3
JEMMY'S SWEARING-IN
MARCH 4, 1809

As Jemmy finally finishes his ten-minute speech that I thought would never end, I force a wide smile and clap. Chief Justice Marshall marches over to administer the oath of office, his enormous body dwarfing Jemmy's slight frame. Just twenty years ago, our first president, General Washington, took the same vow in New York City. How much has transpired in our country since then.

Gritting his teeth, Jemmy raises his right hand and places the left on the Bible.

"Poor Jemmy is scarcely able to stand," Anna whispers, cupping her hand around my ear.

Holding my breath, I grab her hand.

"I do solemnly swear or affirm," recites the Chief Justice in a bold voice that fills the massive room.

Jemmy's mouth moves, forming the same words. Unfortunately, though, I can't hear him, even from a few feet away.

My frustration builds, but I don't dare let it show. Instead, I plaster on a serene smile. Thankfully his voice finally emerges with the last line, "So help me God." Nevertheless, it's official. My husband is now the president of the United

States. This honor comes like a sharpened double-edged sword and just as dangerous.

Politics fascinates me. Regardless of the season, my favorite pastime is attending the passionate debates between the outstanding orators in Congress. It's safe to say that Washington City offers no better entertainment. After all, there's nothing else to do here besides bird watching, but the antics of Polly, my Macaw parrot, amuse me so much more.

I do have an ulterior motive, though. I want to understand the thinking of Jemmy's political foes and cultivate their friendship. The Federalists would like nothing better than to bring him down and then gloat over his demise. I'll do everything in my power to prevent that, all with kind words on my lips and a smile on my face.

Cocking my head, I scan the massive crowd for Jemmy's staunch supporters. The Southern Congressmen huddle together behind me, encircling their handsome leader, Henry Clay of Kentucky. Entranced by his charisma, they elected him Speaker of the House on his first day in office.

Speaker Clay catches my eye and gives me a confident nod of his blond head. He leads a new faction of twelve young Congressmen from the new Western states and the South. Known as the War Hawks, they demand an immediate declaration of war on Great Britain. They fume over the relentless harassment of our sailors and trespassing on our sovereignty as an independent nation.

According to the law of the land, we ladies don't have the right to cast our own votes. In addition, Quakers don't participate in voting to keep us separate from the violence of this fallen world. However, my faith also taught me that men and women are spiritual equals. Even so, I refrain from debating our national policies in public. As Mr. Jefferson once said, "Women are too wise to wrinkle their foreheads with politics." However, I do believe it's time to take action and make sure to tell Jemmy so often.

John Quincy Adams and other angry Doves who oppose the war stand huddled in back, far from former President Jefferson. Their sour expressions do not surprise me in the least. After all, they are the defeated Federalists representing New England and its struggling shipping industry. As Mr. Jefferson's Secretary of State, Jemmy established an embargo that curtailed all trade with Great Britain. The unfortunate result was crippling our own fragile economy, especially the shippers.

Despite all the suffering, though, Britain's evil conduct continues, resulting in many nights of tossing and turning for poor Jemmy. To this day, they persist in snatching our sailors and forcing them to fight in their Royal Navy against Napoleon. They treat us as their subjects, violating our sovereignty. After all, we've been an independent nation since declaring our independence back in 1776. This illegal impressment must stop immediately.

As the ceremony concludes, the Army and Navy bands fill the air with blaring trumpets and pounding drums. My husband's somber gaze lands on me, his blue eyes pooling with warmth. Of course, my heart expands. To this day, I have yet to meet a finer man. Honestly, I still don't feel worthy to be his wife. I want to protect him from the difficulties lying in wait like a pit of vipers, but I can't. All I can do is try to make his life easier by bringing people together. Everyone looks to me for good cheer, especially Jemmy himself.

People love to be loved, especially politicians and their wives, myself included. So, I do my best to love them all. After all, I am dedicated to my country and my husband, plus it's my nature. Although befriending everyone in my path brings me joy, it is not so for my Jemmy. Together, though, we make a wonderful team. I'm honored to use my simple talents, but his vast gifts far outweigh mine. He is truly my better half.

As throngs of people surge in my direction, my sisters and I make our way toward Jemmy. An eager journalist makes a beeline to me and jumps in my path, calling out, "Madam Presidentess!" The jostling crowd copies him, repeating it like an echo.

This tidal wave of attention overwhelms even me, but I greet everyone in turn, lighting up with each interaction. Of course, my exhausted husband would rather retreat home and read his favorite Greek and Latin classics by a roaring fire. I would be happy to oblige, but this day is only beginning. After all, there's nothing I wouldn't do for him. There's nothing I wouldn't do for my country either. Thankfully my two treasured causes lead me along the same path.

CHAPTER 4
OUR RECEPTION
MARCH 4, 1809

L eaving ahead of the masses, Jemmy and I race toward the Senate Chamber in the north wing, avoiding the thousands of well-wishers who await us outside. The plans call for a huge central dome that will connect the two buildings. However, for now there's only a narrow wooden walkway over a mire of mud. The Treasury is out of money.

As we step onto the flimsy boards, Jemmy's thin arm goes around my waist. "Let's take extra care here, my dear. I'm ashamed to tell you this area also serves as the outhouse for Congress."

"So that explains the foul odor. How the Brits would mock us if they knew our vulgar ways." I pinch my nose with one hand and lift my skirt with the other. "And we wonder why they think we are buffoons."

Boom! There's an explosion of some sort. My eyes dart across the dismal field, looking for signs of danger. I lose my balance, and my foot sways toward the mucky abyss.

"Nothing to worry about, my dear," he assures me, pulling me back and reaching up to pat my black curls. "The Navy

Yard and Fort Warburton are firing off their artillery guns. They're just getting started on the celebrations."

Soon we reach our carriage and review the troops in their dress uniforms. Finally, we escape, much to Jemmy's relief. The musicians from the nearby Navy Yard march along to the beat as they escort us back down Pennsylvania Avenue, the only real thoroughfare in Washington City.

With a sigh, Jemmy sinks back and rubs his tired eyes.

I pull the Roman shades all the way up and gaze out the window. "I adore these new poplar trees lining the street."

"Yes, they're a wonderful addition, thanks to Mr. Jefferson," Jemmy agrees. "He's quite a visionary."

"At least they add some sense of pageantry around here." I look over at Jemmy. "But we need so much more."

"One step at a time, my dear," he replies, squeezing my hand.

I frown as we pass the dilapidated boarding houses where our Congressmen live, crammed together with two men per room. A pall descends over us like a storm cloud. "What a dismal existence," I declare. "It's no wonder they all argue without ceasing."

"Yes, the only escape from each other is visiting the outhouse." Jemmy raises his eyebrows. "That's hardly inspiring."

"It's revolting. Washington City has already been our capital for nine years, but it's still such a rural village. Not much has changed since Abigail Adams got lost in the wilderness making her way here from Baltimore."

Next, we gaze out at the oozing swamps interspersed with brickyards and huge piles of rough stones. Every summer mosquitos breed their own armies and wage war on our bodies. Then during the winter, frigid temperatures descend upon us, creating depressing landscapes of frozen mud.

"I have to agree." Jemmy emits a heavy sigh. "It looks

more like a logging camp in the backcountry than the governing seat of a nation."

"Unfortunately, the joke is quite true. Washington City really is streets with no houses, and houses with no streets. Even here on grand Pennsylvania Avenue, there are no buildings."

"Remember our first home here years ago, dearest?" Jemmy's face softens at the memory. "Our address was Six Buildings simply because six buildings stood together."

Clunk! My hip joints hurt with the resounding thud, and we find ourselves stuck in another rut. Poor Paul cannot avoid them despite his best efforts. After all, they're the size of cymbals and everywhere.

"These streets are really just pathways of potholes," I mutter.

Paul looks over his shoulder with a sheepish smile. "Excuse me again, Mr. Madison and Miss Dolley."

Although lost in his thoughts, Jemmy nods. "You're doing a fine job, Paul. I'm just happy to escape the mob." This wonderful man never misses an opportunity to be kind which warms my heart.

Dear Paul has such a gentle way about him, too. He's one of our many slaves, a concept I was raised to abhor as a Quaker. With our blessing, he learned to read and write at our Montpelier Plantation, sitting in on Payne's early lessons. He is also quite talented on the violin.

"Jemmy, you know the crowd will descend on us again once we get home." I pat my husband's hand and give him a rueful smile. Our three-story brick townhouse at 1333 F Street is just two blocks from the President's House.

"I'm resigned to that. I'm just savoring these moments of quiet, even if they are bumpy." He stretches out his legs and holds my hand for the rest of the ride, our fingers intertwined.

Indeed, an onslaught of company descends upon us within minutes of our arrival back home, much to my delight and Jemmy's dismay. Carriages flood the street, creating a bottle-neck. Even more well-wishers clog the sidewalk to gawk at us. Soon throngs of people push their way inside, and our house overflows as well. The entryway, parlor, drawing room, and even our bedroom spill over with countless strangers, fellow citizens, and friends.

I am so grateful for my dignified doorman, Jean Pierre Sioussat of France, whom I hired from President Jefferson's staff. At only twelve-years-old, he witnessed the beheadings of both King Louis XVI and Marie Antoinette during the Reign of Terror. When his aristocratic parents died soon afterwards, he became a ward of the church and then a seminarian. Finally, he joined the French Navy. Upon sailing into New York City, he jumped ship and swam ashore. Then he made his way to Washington City and worked for Mr. Jefferson.

Known as French John, this tall and stately man estab-lishes order with firm rules and impeccable decorum. He even succeeds in holding back the next wave of eager visitors for almost an hour, waiting for the crowd to thin out. This is no easy feat since no one wants to leave, but his charming French accent proves quite an asset.

Thankfully our servants handle the mass of humanity descending upon us with great skill. Paul and Sukey, my young maid, grit their teeth amidst the constant jostling as they offer tasty refreshments from ornate silver trays. No spills occur, which is a relief. I dread Sukey's frustration more than any actual damage.

She may be only fourteen-years-old, but Sukey's domestic abilities are excellent. I do my best to tolerate her tempera-mental behavior. It's no secret she misses her family back at Montpelier, causing a terrible ache in her heart. I regret that our situation requires this long separation from her loved ones. At her adolescent age, I can't imagine the pain. Fortunately for everyone's sake, Paul seems better able to handle it.

In addition to many tasks in the kitchen down below, Sukey cares for my wardrobe, helps me dress several times a day, and even styles my hair with great expertise. Since she and Paul were both born at Montpelier, they've known each other all their lives. To their credit, they get along better than most siblings.

Inside the front door, I greet our curious callers with aplomb. Perched on my shoulder, my bright green parrot squawks, "Congratulations, Mr. President!" I laugh, confident Polly is the spunkiest parrot on this earth. Thank goodness she is mine, despite her rowdy ways. Oh, what a racket this girl can make!

My bashful husband stands next to me with a tortured expression and his hands clasped behind him. He doesn't make a wonderful first impression as our new president, but I hope my enthusiasm makes up for it. Nevertheless, whenever a guest finally departs, Jemmy bends over in a low bow like he's back at dancing school. Despite his utter exhaustion, he remains gallant.

"I'm so sorry you're going home," I murmur in each ear. Truly I am. The bigger the crowd around me, the happier I am.

Eventually Congressman Randolph makes his way through the line in his usual flashy outfit. "Dolley and Polly, how clever," he blusters with a roll of his eyes. Quakers believe all people are vessels of God, but his obnoxious behavior makes me wonder. Perhaps some human vessels contain only sin.

Fixing her eyes on him, Polly lets out a screech and ruffles her brilliant green feathers. I reach up and pet her while I choke back a guffaw. She's an excellent judge of character and known to dive-bomb at people whom she dislikes. Although I am tempted to encourage her, I must settle her down or she will upstage us all.

To our surprise, Mr. Jefferson is next in line to greet us. I should have known he'd wait in the queue like everyone else. He frowns as he shakes Jemmy's hand. "Please excuse Congressman Randolph, Mr. President. It appears my cousin left his gentlemanly manners back home in Virginia once again."

I smile as he kisses both my cheeks according to French etiquette. "Really, Mr. Jefferson! Shouldn't you be back at the President's House receiving your own houseful of guests?"

"Oh, I'm just a squatter there now. America's real leader is here." He opens his hands, gesturing to Jemmy.

With a grin, Speaker Clay steps forward. "You look so happy and satisfied, Mr. Jefferson. Mr. Madison looks so serious and rather sad. A spectator might think you are the one coming into office, and he is going out."

"There's good reason for my happy and his serious mood." Mr. Jefferson winks. "The burden has been taken off my shoulders, and now he's got it on his. Never did a prisoner, released from his chains, feel such relief as I do in shaking off the shackles of power. The presidency is splendid misery, but I wish my friend the best."

CHAPTER 5

AMERICA'S FIRST INAUGURAL BALL

MARCH 4, 1809

Not long after the last dilly-dallier finally leaves, we must dress for tonight's Inaugural Ball. I'm full of anticipation since this will be the first celebration of its kind for our country. Everyone is welcome to attend provided they can afford the pricey four-dollar ticket. We must celebrate or at least make the appearance of it. The Federalists will scrutinize our every move for signs of weakness. Therefore, I plan to display nothing but positivity.

"Must we do this tonight, my darling?" Jemmy muses. "Our first three presidents ended their first days in office by retiring early. How I would love to honor their tradition." He gives a low chuckle.

"Nonsense, Jemmy!" I scold him with a smile. Of course, his lack of interest does not surprise me at all. "The Europeans have their lavish festivities, and we Americans need to develop some grandeur for ourselves. But I do promise to leave early."

"As you wish, my dear." Jemmy nods. "In that case, I'm ready to go, especially since I'm wearing my one and only suit."

"I am so fortunate you don't hold me to the same standard. Sometimes I wonder if you are the real Quaker here." I can't resist teasing him, but I am no longer a member of the Religious Society of Friends. According to its strict rules, the church cast me out when I married Jemmy, an outsider.

In contrast to the plain dress code of my youth, my love of French fashion is no secret. I especially adore the high style of Napoleon Bonaparte's wife, the elegant Empress Josephine who also comes from humble beginnings. Nothing excites me more than receiving a new fashion doll straight from Paris, clad in a miniature version of their latest trend. Then I put my seamstress to work, adapting the dress to my plump size.

"But my best part of all is wearing turbans. Then I tower over the crowd, and you can see me from anywhere in the room. You're much harder to find since you're usually huddled in a dark corner in your black suit."

"And so happy to be there," Jemmy reminds me with a wink.

I give him a playful swat as Sukey bustles into the room. First, she delivers piping hot coffee on a tray. She returns a few minutes later, carrying my pale yellow gown in her outstretched arms. She's even looped the lengthy train lined with rich purple velvet around her shoulders. As she lays it out on the bed, I beam, already anticipating the attention that I will receive tonight. Then, she scurries in a third time, now holding up my quilted corset.

"Excuse me, Miss Dolley, but we best start getting you ready now. We don't have much time. Paul's already gone to the stables to fetch the carriage."

I sigh, resigned to the next step. Ah, the corset is my enemy, but a necessary one. After all, it allows me to indulge in my favorite cakes daily. As Sukey laces me up, I pretend it squeezes my fears away. If only that was true!

Soon I am fully dressed, and Sukey presses the turban down onto my loose black curls. Once she pins it into place, I splash a heavy dose of lilac perfume on my neck and then douse my wrists. In an instant the floral fragrance soothes my jangled nerves. It's nothing short of a miracle drug, even better than tobacco snuff for me. Then I pinch my fair cheeks for some fresh color. Lastly, I add a generous helping of rouge and blot it with pearl powder dust. With a thick layer of red lipstick, I am ready at last.

In a dazzling burst of bright green, Polly flies into the room and lands on my shoulder. She nuzzles my neck and coos in her shrill voice, "Mrs. Madison is beautiful."

"Thank you, Polly. Now it's time to show off our feathers, too." I stroke her colorful plumes as her long tail tickles my shoulder blade.

"*Voila!* Now where is our new President Madison?" I call, bursting out of my dressing room.

Startled, Polly flies off in a huff while I grab the skirt of the velvet gown made in my favorite French style. Meanwhile Sukey lunges at its elegant train, preventing it from catching on the doorway. "Miss Dolley, you are going to tear this dress before you even leave the house."

I force myself to smile. I try to meet her bouts of crankiness with patience. Fashion is pure pleasure for me, but for her it just means additional work. I so depend on her help, especially when feeling lonely or depressed. I cannot hide my woes from her. Only she knows the constant pain of rheumatism in my sad knee and sometimes my shoulder, too. I don't want to worry Jemmy, but it often hurts even to raise my arm.

As I walk down the staircase with a firm grip on the handrail, Jemmy awaits me below. Sukey matches my steps as she carries my train. "Behold Queen Dolley! You certainly make up for your Quaker youth with such flamboyant style." He gestures to my yellow velvet and silk headpiece with tall bird-of-paradise feathers jutting into the air. "That's quite a crown you wear, my dear Presidentess." He takes a step back and ponders. "Such interesting spikes. Did you borrow my quills? I noticed a few are missing."

I can't help but giggle, and so does he. Ah, my darling husband knows me so well. "Well, here in America, we don't believe in crowns. But I do believe in turbans. And the more glamorous, the better. I'll have you know these gorgeous feathers came all the way from Fiji."

"I spent two hours curling them," Sukey mutters under her breath. "They better look mighty pretty."

Although tempted to chide her, I decide to ignore her grumbling and compliment her instead. "Sukey, you've done such a wonderful job today. It's well after dusk, so please have yourself some supper. And take tomorrow morning to yourself." With a curtsy and a nod, she is gone.

"Jemmy, I have you to thank—you saved me from the drudgery of somber dress." Now at the bottom of the stairs, I put one hand on his arm and take the rope of pearls from my pocket. "Before I forget, will you please fasten these?"

"An excellent choice, my dear." He gives me a playful wink and winds them around my neck. "Quite tasteful and elegant. And they match your earrings and bracelet as well."

"I was wondering when you'd notice." I widen my eyes with a coquettish smile.

"No doubt you'll set off another fashion trend tonight." He muses in his low voice. "All the American ladies will be wearing pearls to formal events for centuries to come, wanting to be just like you."

"I can only hope so, for I love the modesty of pearls. Diamonds are far too regal. They just smack of the British aristocracy. We fought in the Revolution to break away from that."

"Excellent point, my dear," Jemmy agrees. "Clothing can

indeed convey messages, but yours are definitely more interesting than mine."

Upon our eight o'clock arrival at the lovely Long's Hotel on Capitol Hill, Margaret Bayard Smith of the *National Intelligencer* greets us with pecks on the cheek and nervous chatter in the lobby. "Oh, my dear Dolley, you look utterly ravishing, just like a queen. Such dignity and grace I've never seen." She gestures toward the ballroom. "Now go ahead and look. I've never seen such a dense crowd in all my life. Four hundred people are gathered here, just to take a gander at you."

Margaret reaches out, shielding me with her arm. "Be careful, though, we can't let anyone see you or there'll be a stampede." She purses her lips and shakes her head. "That wouldn't look good in the paper tomorrow."

As we sneak a peek inside, the mass of guests takes my breath away. It would be impossible to even elbow your way across the room. Jemmy and I stare, equally amazed.

"Your admirers await you, Mrs. Madison. I am merely your escort," he quips with a wry smile.

There's some truth to that, but some are here to seek his patronage as our brand-new president. Still, he makes me chuckle. "I certainly hope a fire doesn't break out or we're all doomed," I respond.

"I take offense to that. I'm supposed to be the dour one," Jemmy says with a wink.

I break out in a cackle. If only the world knew his wonderful humor like I do.

From the shadows, our red-headed friend emerges and rests his hand on Jemmy's back. "G-g-g-g-good evening, Mr. President." As usual, Mr. Jefferson's voice is soft and comes with a slight stutter.

"Good evening to you, too, Mr. Jefferson." Jemmy replies, looking up at him. Their height difference is almost a foot, but they are both intellectual giants in my eyes.

"Indeed, it is. Back to my favorite title of all–American citizen." Mr. Jefferson beams and kisses both my cheeks in the French style. "Mrs. Madison, my dear friend, am I too early? Please, you must tell me how to behave tonight. It's been more than forty years since I've been to a ball."

I laugh, but before I can respond, the Marine Corps Band strikes up 'Mr. Jefferson's March.' Mr. Jefferson hesitates for a moment as if tempted to run away. Then he shrugs and saunters off into the ballroom with his usual slumped shoulders. The crowd breaks into an enthusiastic round of applause and shuffles to make a narrow pathway for him.

When 'Mr. Madison's March' starts up next, Jemmy and I link arms and stroll into the sweltering ballroom, practically rubbing up against our guests. He whispers, "Bah!" into my ear, setting me laughing once again. If I can be strong in his few areas of weakness, that brings me such joy. I owe him so much more for all he's done for my precious Payne and me. I'd do anything to make his presidency successful.

Unfortunately, the band concludes just as a country matron shrieks, "Why, look at his wrinkled face! He's no bigger than half a piece of soap, while she moves like a goddess, floating along like a queen. Surely they are the oddest couple in the world."

"Did you see the bodice on her dress? She's showing her bosom off to the world!" shouts another outraged woman.

My jaw tightens, and Jemmy winces. Alas, we carry on, like we always do. Immediately people swarm around me like bees to a hive. They push in from all sides, peeping and gawking at me. I feel like a rare doll on display in a store window.

The same surging sea of well-wishers swallows up Jemmy and carries him off. I keep an airy smile plastered on my face as they stomp on my delicate train with their mud-caked shoes. I give it a sharp tug, hoping to free myself. Instead, there's a horrible tearing sound. Heaven, help me, I'm trapped and already dreading Sukey's reaction to the destruction of her precise stitching.

As the event continues, the heat grows more oppressive. Still, no one has any desire to depart. Rouge drips down my face, landing in rosy droplets on my precious French gown. How I would love to have a fan right now! Soon I fear the curious crowd will press me to death, despite their best intentions.

Within a minute, the room has no air. I can't breathe, but I keep smiling anyway. Our desperate guests stand together on benches, seeking relief. Others pound on the windows, but they're painted shut. Soon a few ladies faint, swooning onto the guests pressed in around them. Finally, some Congressmen grab chairs and smash open the windows with a series of thunderous crashes. Jagged shards of glass lie scattered about, sparkling like extravagant jewels on people's shoulders. Alas, everyone is too busy gulping in the cool fresh air to care about any damage, myself included.

Alas, my spiritless husband is nowhere to be found. After pushing my way into every dark corner, I eventually discover him huddled on a chair with dear Margaret interviewing him for the *National Intelligencer*. The poor man is bone-tired, as well he should be.

"I would much rather be asleep," he whispers with a wan smile.

Fortunately, dinner is soon served, but political obligations soon make the scrumptious meal that I planned far less appetizing. I am seated between the French Minister named General Louis-Marie Turreau de Garambouville and the British Minister, David Montague Erskine.

Abandoning the usual niceties right away, the British Minister launches the first missile at his adversary. "So, when will Napoleon give up on his delusions of grandeur?" he muses with a smug smile.

"Bah! But he is no longer Napoleon." The French Minister tosses his head and curls his lip. "He is the Emperor of the French. Our Emperor is a military genius, and the French Empire dominates all of Europe."

"I can assure you, his fiefdom won't last much longer," sneers Minister Erskine. "We will soon teach him to accept his place in the world and send him back to his humble roots in Corsica."

Alas, these accomplished diplomats could not be any less diplomatic. I cannot decide which one irks me more. Although I want to throttle them both, I summon every charm left at my disposal to get through the meal. No dueling takes place, so Jemmy and I consider it a grand success.

When the dancing commences, we decline. With my deep Quaker roots, I never learned how, and the swelling in my knee makes it impossible. Needless to say, Jemmy was in no mood for such frivolity either. He appears quite content in the corner conferring with Speaker Clay.

"Mrs. Madison, who pray tell is this lady over here?" asks a handsome War Hawk from Tennessee, but he doesn't bother to look at me. Instead, he gazes starry-eyed at the exceptional beauty with her dark hair and light eyes, surrounded by suitors on the dance floor.

"You're definitely new in town if you don't recognize my dear friend." I laugh. "That's Betsy Bonaparte."

"Oh, so she is the legendary Belle of Baltimore!" He nods, still staring at her, mesmerized. "She's even more eye-catching than I've heard." He finally tears his eyes away to look at me. "But isn't she married to Napoleon's youngest brother? The Lieutenant in the French Navy?"

"Well, she and Jerome *were* happily married." I tilt my head, pausing to collect my thoughts on this delicate situation. Of course, I want to present my friend in the best possible light.

I continue, "However, Napoleon declared their union illegitimate despite the fact that she was in the family way. Then he forced Jerome to marry Princess Catharina of Wurttemberg, a German Kingdom. Now they reign as King and Queen of Wurttemberg."

Clasp my hands together, I beam. "And we are so fortunate to have Betsy and her son Beau here with us." I so admire how poor Betsy suffered this humiliation in front of the entire world but handled it with such grace. She still insists on using the surname Bonaparte despite Napoleon's pressure to abandon it.

"So, you are saying the Belle is single again?" A mischievous grin spreads across his face.

"Indeed, she is. As you can see, she has many eager admirers if you care to step in line. But no matter how smitten you are, don't get your hopes up. She vows never to make herself beholden to another man."

"If you'll excuse me, Mrs. Madison, I shall do my best to change her mind," he replies with a smirk.

"Best of luck to you, Congressman," I call to his retreating back.

☙❧

THE CELEBRATION WILL CONTINUE UNTIL MIDNIGHT. However, we soon work our way out of the massive throngs to depart, much to my husband's delight. As we bid our goodbyes, John Quincy Adams emerges from the festive crowd and mutters in my ear, "The crowd was excessive, the heat was oppressive, and the entertainment bad." I enjoy a good laugh. His stiffness reminds me so much of his father, former

President John Adams, but he makes a wonderful diplomat, even as a Federalist.

Margaret guides us out the back door with an expert hand, raving about the evening. "You were absolutely radiant tonight! I can't wait to write it up for the paper tomorrow. This has been the most brilliant event in Washington City society!"

"As if that means anything," Jemmy quips.

She and I smile and shake our heads, exchanging knowing looks.

Back in the carriage, Jemmy yawns and then grabs my hand. "Ah, I was the envy of all tonight."

"Jemmy, you've just taken on the hardest job in the world." I scoff. "No one in their right mind would be jealous, not with war with Britain looming on the horizon."

"Yes, but I'm married to the Lady Presidentess."

"But we both know the truth. I am the lucky one." I give him a peck on the cheek.

Once we arrive back home, I hide my damaged gown at the back of my wardrobe. There's no need to add extra work for Sukey. After all, I have no plans to wear this dress again, not anytime soon.

"Ah, the best part of the day." Jemmy mutters as blows out the candle. "Please pray for me, my darling."

"Always," I whisper back. As a slew of worries flood my mind, America's new president drifts off into a fitful sleep.

CHAPTER 6
VISITING THE PRESIDENT'S HOUSE

LATE MARCH 1809

When dear Mr. Jefferson finally departs two weeks later for his cherished Monticello in Charlottesville, Jemmy and I take an uneasy ride to the President's House, our new home. We are both quite familiar with the dismal state of America's largest residence. Of course, I don't want to burden Jemmy with my sour thoughts, so I keep them to myself. Perhaps he enjoys the rare reprieve from my usual chatter. However, he is far too kind-hearted to ever admit it.

The barren vistas along the short route make my heart ache for bustling Philadelphia where we spent the early years of our marriage. It's such a gentrified city, unlike this pitiful town. After the war, my father freed our slaves and moved us there from Scotchtown Plantation in Hanover County, Virginia. Quakers don't believe in owning other human beings since each person has an inner light. Unfortunately, his noble decision to move our family to the largest Quaker city created a severe financial hardship.

When Father's new starch business failed, the Religious

Society of Friends disowned him, casting him out as a "stranger." Devastated, he took to his bed until he died. Left with few options, Mother converted our home into a boardinghouse. Philadelphia served as the capital during the construction of Washington City. Senator Aaron Burr of New York became our tenant and then introduced me to Jemmy, the beloved third-term Congressman from Virginia, Father of the Constitution, and drafter of the Bill of Rights.

General Washington was so fortunate. He chose the location for Washington City near his home at Mount Vernon and oversaw the first cornerstone laid for the President's House. However, he never had to actually live in this dreadful swamp. Of course, I can never utter such thoughts aloud, not even to my sisters. I must put forth nothing but unbridled enthusiasm for the vast potential of our new capital city, regardless of my true feelings.

John Adams, our second president, and his wife Abigail only spent their last few months in the "Great Castle." It was still under construction, so they couldn't furnish it. Then when Mr. Jefferson moved in, he concentrated on frugality and practical measures. He spent the funds allotted by Congress on improving the roof, outfitting the kitchen, and installing basic items like window blinds and floor cloths.

Ever full of gallantry, Jemmy holds my elbow as we make our way through the sea of squishy mud to the ominous front door. Sukey stands off to the side, holding the train of my gauzy dress aloft. A dedicated servant, she ignores the muck rising around her ankles. However, she frowns when it seeps up around my white embroidered slippers. After all, she is responsible for cleaning them. Heavens, I can't imagine what I'd do without her.

Nothing about the President's House is complete, not even the front steps. Now viewing it through the eyes of a new occupant, I want to break into sobs, but only allow myself to sigh. Piles of lumber, bricks, and stones lay scattered everywhere. There are no gates or shrubbery, only Mr. Jefferson's rough sheep fence that surrounds some huge stumps with moats of lumpy mud.

I shudder, praying our dreadful surroundings won't bother Jemmy as much as me. I need not have worried though. He just moves forward, as placid as ever, and we make our way across the rough ground. To his credit, he doesn't sulk over life's obstacles—one of his many admirable qualities. At least having Lucy and her boys living here with us will help make it feel more like a real home.

As we reach the front door, Jemmy grasps the ornate knob, far larger than his small palm. I muster a smile. At least the President's House has one redeeming feature. This is a doorknob worthy of the United States of America. I want to hope that this bodes well for the interior, but I know better. When we first arrived in Washington City, we stayed here with Mr. Jefferson for weeks before moving into Six Buildings. Back then it was just a brand-new shell, still reeking of plaster.

Since Mr. Jefferson is a widower, I presided over many intimate dinners here as his happy hostess. At first the society women scoffed at me, calling me "common." They were outraged that I paint my face with rouge, enjoy tobacco snuff, play cards, and gamble. Of course, my revealing Empire-waist gowns in gauzy fabrics also offended their sensibilities, as well as my glamorous headdresses. Soon enough, though, my surging popularity silenced them. Then my thoughtful overtures transformed them into lifelong friends. Nowadays no one wears bulky petticoats, hoop skirts, or uncomfortable stays anymore, not even them.

When we enter the building, the sorry condition inside

still shocks me. It's far drearier than I recalled. The bare walls are in desperate need of paint, stained by the leaky roof. Our muddy footsteps echo throughout the depressing rooms, reflecting the hollowness of my heart. I bite my lip to keep myself from complaining aloud to Jemmy.

We step into the huge oval drawing room where Abigail Adams used to hang her laundry. Almost no furnishings or décor remain. What little exists is threadbare, especially the crimson damask settee and chairs. Although red is my favorite color, this dowdy set is twenty years old and makes me shudder. The one saving grace is the small bronze clock that Mrs. Adams left behind for posterity. I am so grateful for her contribution, one of America's first heirlooms.

Mr. Jefferson took his lovely possessions and fascinating artifacts from the Lewis and Clark Expedition back to Monticello with him, and rightly so. However, that leaves us in quite a lurch. It's a pitiful sight, most unsuitable for our head of state. Like it or not, though, this disheveled mess is my new residence. Even worse, I am now responsible for its status of disrepair. How mortifying.

I gaze out the window at President's Park across the way, one of the few parks established in Washington City. Unfortunately, in reality it is an abandoned apple orchard with some crooked gravestones in the corner. Like all the land here, it's brown, gooey, and downright repulsive.

"Jemmy, this place is in shambles." My outrage finally bubbles over, and I huff, "The President's Palace is anything but that. It looks more like a rundown home for paupers."

"You're right." He nods, putting a hand to his chin. "It does."

"We must do something about it, right away." I look him in the eye, challenging him.

"Well, there aren't many options." Jemmy's voice is tense. "Congress won't give us any money, not with our finances so tight right now." He surveys the bleak rooms and shakes his head. "It would cost much more than my salary to make this whole house presentable. After all, my pay is quite high— $25,000.

I purse my lips and frown.

"Don't worry, my dear," he reassures me. "It's just a place for us to relax at the end of the day. We'll muddle through somehow; we can make do."

"Make do? We must thrive, and our country must, too." I let out an exasperated sigh.

Thankfully the perfect idea comes to me. "Jemmy, would you please arrange for Speaker Clay and the Congressmen who hold the purse strings to meet me here tomorrow morning? I'd like to take them on a tour. I'm in a better position to shame them into giving us a reasonable budget to decorate. This place desperately needs some dignity, especially the front rooms."

"Yes, my dear, as you wish." With a wink, he bows. "I am at your service as your faithful servant."

"And I'm going to call on Mr. Latrobe this afternoon and ask him to work with me." I put my hands on my hips. "As the architect of the Capitol, he's perfect for the job. Just you wait, the President's House will be a sight to behold. It'll be the talk of the town!"

"I have no doubt, my dearest. If anyone can make this happen, it's you."

I beam in response, wondering why people can't understand why I love him so.

Next, we stroll into Mr. Jefferson's former study and then stop in our tracks, dumbfounded by the beauty in front of us. The stunning portrait of America's first president lay propped against the stained wall. Wearing a simple black suit, General Washington looms large as life. The famous artist Gilbert Stuart depicted him at his full height of six foot three inches during the last year of his presidency, standing between columns as if giving a speech. With one hand holding a sword, the other stretches out in peace.

"I will find the perfect spot for this!" I declare.

"Of that, I have no doubt," Jemmy replies with a wink.

CHAPTER 7
MY CHARM OFFENSIVE
LATE MARCH 1809

When Speaker Henry Clay pounds on the front door the next morning, the sound bounces off the empty walls of the President's House. However, I make him and his group of fellow Congressmen wait outside. Whether they realize it or not, they need some time to take in the deplorable condition of the grounds.

After ten minutes or so, I finally open the door with a wide smile. "Thank you so much for coming, Congressmen. I'm so sorry, I didn't hear you knocking. It's such a lovely treat having you all here today, especially on such short notice."

"Mrs. Madison, I can assure you, it is entirely our pleasure." Speaker Clay gives a slight bow to me, oozing with his usual charm.

"Mrs. Calhoun also sends her kind regards," offers John C. Calhoun of South Carolina, tipping his head toward me.

"Thank you so much, Mr. Calhoun. Please do send her my love."

Then I turn to address the group. "Well, gentlemen, I know you're awfully busy, so I won't take much of your time.

Please take a good look around you." I raise my arm, leading them into the barren oval drawing room. "America is a young country, and we definitely don't believe in monarchies. However, I hope we can all agree that we do need some pomp. Let's keep in mind that King George III lives in Buckingham Palace, and Napoleon at Versailles. They wear crowns covered with jewels and sit on gilded thrones, not shabby chairs like these."

In one swift motion, I fold my arms and sink down into a faded crimson chair left by Abigail Adams. As if to prove my point, it wobbles and emits a dreadful groan while a cloud of gray particles rises. "Gentlemen, perhaps I've eaten too much rich food of late, but this is entirely unacceptable."

The Speaker chuckles as I wave away the dust. I'm tempted to laugh along with him, but I refrain and frown instead. The others wince.

"Yes, we see your point, Mrs. Madison, but..."

My glare silences the Speaker mid-sentence, but then he continues. "Really, I do. But the Treasury is practically bare as it is. We need to save every penny for the war."

"Speaker Clay, our finances may be in dismal shape, but America needs to maintain an appearance of prosperity." I throw up my hands. "After all, how else will we earn the respect of the people and the entire world? Our president should not live in these pitiful conditions. It's a disgrace. We do agree that he shouldn't live like a king either. However, the President's House should represent the dignity of the office, similar to the opulence of the Capitol. We can't put a price on our national pride."

"Mrs. Madison, I wholeheartedly agree. You're absolutely right—it definitely needs to be addressed. " He waves his hands. "But can't these lovely decorating ideas wait until after we win the war? We're all War Hawks here, and we know it'll be over in a flash. Even Mr. Jefferson says it'll be a mere matter of marching to liberate Canada from the British."

"This war will be a favorite with the country," declares Congressman Calhoun with a fierce look in his glowing dark eyes. "Much honor awaits those who will distinguish themselves in combat. But they must do it fast before it's over."

"Think about it, Congressmen." I have not come this far to give up now, so I launch into a rant. "What message does this send our enemies? No wonder Britain and France thrash us about like a cat toying with a dead mouse. I have no doubt their foreign ministers have reported on the embarrassing condition of this house, not to mention our desolate capital city."

I pause to make eye contact with each and every one of them. "Gentlemen, they believe we are poor and weak. And no, it cannot wait." I shake my head for effect. "Our grand experiment with liberty fascinates the world. Many believe that failure is inevitable. We must prove them wrong. We must transform this abysmal shell into a triumphant symbol of American progress."

They remain silent, trading sidelong glances with each other. I don't want to press my luck, but I must get them to commit now while I have them in my midst.

"I've already enlisted the services of Mr. Latrobe who designed the Capitol." Putting a hand to my heart, I smile. "And we promise to stick to a reasonable budget."

"As you wish, Mrs. Madison." With a heavy sigh, Speaker Clay hangs his head and then raises it, looking me in the eye. "Will $5,000 be enough?"

"Oh, Mr. Speaker! How wonderful." I'm thrilled. After all, I didn't expect him to offer nearly that much. "Yes, that will be plenty; I will make sure of it. I can't thank you enough," I respond as the other lawmakers stare down at their grimy shoes.

In addition to improving the state of the house itself, my mind churns with other lofty ideas. Perhaps we can use our new abode to reduce the notorious mudslinging in Washington City. Of course, I can't do anything about the actual mud in this swamp of a town. However, I can launch a charm offensive against the great political divide that pits the the Republicans and Federalists against each other.

My first step is to confer with my most influential friend other than Jemmy. Of course, that is Margaret at the helm of the *National Intelligencer,* alongside her husband. We enjoy a social cup of coffee on the stylish new settee in my parlor, doing our best to ignore the unpleasant smell of wet paint that plagues us. Since our second boycott of British tea began a few years ago, coffee has become our national drink.

"Dolley, I just adore the yellow you've put in here. It brightened my mood just walking in. And this upholstery is gorgeous, too." She runs her finger along the sleek silk. "You have such exquisite taste."

"Why, thank you so much, honey. Mr. Latrobe and I have been trying to find the finest materials." I chuckle. "Then we insist on the best prices, of course."

"Ah, it's such a treat to come here and visit with you."

"Margaret, I have an idea to share with you, and would love your thoughts on it." I take a sip of coffee and nibble on some Woodbury cinnamon tea cake, still warm from the oven.

"Do tell." She sets down her mug and leans toward me with an indulgent smile.

"Well, as you know, our Congressmen have to live in those wretched boardinghouses without the company of their families."

"Yes, and they do nothing but bicker about politics night and day." She shakes her head. "It's awful."

"Well, I'd like to give them a lovely place to gather, so they can get to know each other as people."

"What a wonderful idea, Dolley." She smiles. "But where do you propose to hold it? We're so strapped for meeting space, especially for such a large group."

Before I can think of the best way to phrase it, I burst out, "Right here, of course!"

"Here? In the President's House?" She tilts her head. "What an interesting concept."

"Well, it wouldn't be just the Congressmen. We would open up the drawing rooms to everyone."

"Everyone?" Margaret raises her eyebrows. "Yes, everyone in Washington City is invited." I give a firm nod, adding, "Including the ladies."

"Really? The ladies, too?" Margaret claps her hands together, and her face lights up. "You've got my curiosity now."

"Yes, we're all Americans, and this house belongs to all of us."

"How wonderful. Heavens, I love this notion. When you're ready, would you let me run an advertisement in the paper?"

"Why, what a wonderful help!" I feign surprise. "I'd be so honored. Thank you, my sweet friend!"

My next step is to convince the president, and I don't delay. As soon as Margaret departs, I venture upstairs to Jemmy's office where he takes copious notes from several open volumes. He's so engrossed in his work that he doesn't notice me. After several minutes, he finally looks up and smiles, startled to see me standing there.

"Jemmy, it's admirable that you don't accept any dinner invitations. Of course, you don't want to show favoritism, the same as General Washington. But you don't get the chance to speak with the people, and they don't get to meet you."

"As you know, that's no sacrifice on my part, my dear." He puts down his quill. "In fact, I consider it a blessing. You know how much I despise chit-chat. I'd rather be right here in the company of my library." He relaxes back in his chair. "After all, you mingle plenty for both of us."

"But Jemmy, we live in a republic. Our president should make himself available to the citizens who want to talk to him."

"That's a lofty concept, but it's just not possible." He gestures down to the overflowing piles on his desk. "I'd have constant interruptions all day, leaving no time to do any actual work."

"Yes, but the people want to know you."

"Well, what do you propose?" He smiles. "I sense you are bursting with a brilliant idea."

"Let's schedule a time every week to open up the drawing rooms to anyone who wants to come visit."

"Visit here?" Jemmy raises his eyebrows.

"Yes, exactly, the President's House." I give a firm nod.

"Well, Jefferson didn't entertain here much." He shrugs. "So, I figure we don't need to either."

"I love our absentminded friend dearly, but greeting visitors in farmer clothes and slippers with holes in the toes hasn't gained us the respect of the populace—or the rest of the world." I gape at him, incredulous. "That's what we desperately need. Of course, he's quite shy, but he only opened up the house to visitors on New Year's Day and the Fourth of July."

"Well, he wanted to avoid elaborate celebrations to show the world that we aren't a monarchy." He shrugs. "He was trying to avoid appearing like a pretentious royal court."

Pursing my lips together, I stare at him and wait.

He looks down at the treatises on his desk and then back up at me.

"Perhaps he took his democratic simplicity a bit too far," he finally mutters, breaking the uncomfortable silence. "But dearest, do you really think people would come? Especially the Federalists? They despise us, and we can't even trust them to act with proper decorum. Can you imagine how the Brits would laugh if a duel broke out right here in the President's House?"

"There won't be any duels, I can guarantee you that." I give a determined nod. "After all, people behave as well as you treat them. We shall welcome every American to our drawing rooms as long as they're in their best attire, whatever that may be. Then we'll entertain them all as treasured guests in our home, whether they're Speaker Clay or his coachman. Of course, the ladies are welcome as well. I just spoke with Margaret at length, and she's quite excited. She's even offered to run an announcement in the paper for us."

"Ah, I see. It appears the Lady Presidentess has done her research. Who am I to stand in your way?" Jemmy's eyes twinkle. "Are you aware, my dear, many of these coachmen have never used a fork or held a porcelain cup?"

"Then they shall learn it here at the President's House, even if I must teach them myself." I raise my index finger. "I can promise you this: our guests will leave here happier than when they arrived."

"I trust your instincts better than my own, especially when it comes to people. I was never well enough to be a soldier, so I'll let you lead the charge." Jemmy grins. "Let your charm offensive begin, my dear." Standing up, he makes a feeble attempt to curtsy. Then he almost topples over, sending me into gales of laughter.

When I finally catch my breath, I play along. "Sometimes even we Quakers must take up arms at some point, just like

General Greene during the War of Independence." I still admire the Fighting Quaker.

"Of course, Betsy is at the top of my guest list." My face brightens. "If she comes, then the crowds will follow. The men will be so busy ogling her they'll forget to argue about politics. No doubt her revealing dress will set the ladies' tongues wagging yet again."

"Good for her," he declares in a light tone. "She deserves the attention after everything she's endured. I'm sure that with both you and Betsy as a draw, we'll have half of Washington City here gawking."

"That will be just the start, Mr. President. Mark my words!" I wag my index finger at him. "With my budget from Congress, Mr. Latrobe and I will focus on decorating the three front drawing rooms. I plan to blend our Republican preference for simplicity with the Federalist taste for high fashion. Our living quarters are not important, not right now. This is our national home, and I want everyone to know it belongs to them."

TWO WEEKS LATER, I TROT UP TO JEMMY'S STUDY AFTER A rare Cabinet meeting concludes. I can tell by his clenched teeth that he is irritated. The men who are supposed to support him only add to his frustration. To cheer him up, I rave about our decorating progress, exclaiming, "Mr. Latrobe and I even chose the perfect spot for the portrait of General Washington in the oval drawing room. I can't wait to see it on display there!"

Jemmy frowns, and I already regret broaching the subject now. "My dear, if you don't mind me saying so, I believe it would be better suited in the dining room. Then the entire room would focus on it. Our guests could sit back and study it over a lengthy meal rather than just glancing at it while chatting."

"But Mr. Latrobe and I made the decision to hang it in the oval room." I'm rather taken aback, and my voice turns a bit frosty.

"I'm sorry, my dear, but I don't agree," Jemmy persists, much to my dismay.

"May I remind you that you left these decisions to me?" I put my hands on my round hips, ready for a rare spat. "Mr. Latrobe and I spent hours discussing the options in painstaking detail."

"Yes, but..." Jemmy interjects.

"Well, that's what we decided on—the oval room." I remain firm.

"I know how hard you've worked." Jemmy looks away. "And I hate to disagree with you, but I have to insist."

"As you wish, Mr. President." I glare at him. "But just remember, this is a final decision. The frame is exquisite. However, it is also quite heavy, even heavier than me after feasting on a tray of sweets. It certainly can't hang from wires, so French John will have to screw it to the wall using a stepladder. Should you change your mind, it will be a quite an ordeal to remove it."

"I'm quite sure." Jemmy musters a smile. "Thank you for indulging me. I promise to leave the rest to you."

"And I shall hold you to that," I reply.

CHAPTER 8
WEDNESDAY-NIGHT DRAWING ROOMS

MAY 1809

Only two months after Jemmy's inauguration, I am ready. I can't wait to open our exquisite drawing rooms for our fellow citizens to enjoy. Mr. Latrobe and I decorated them with rapt attention to every detail. Finally, we Americans can take pride in our national homestead. My dream is for the President's House to become the center of society here in Washington City.

Our dear French John deserves heaps of credit. His childhood spent growing up in the grand Parisian Royal Court provides a wonderful resource as we develop our young American regime. I could not be more pleased to call him my friend, he who has a gift for pleasing everyone, especially me. This cultured man is never at a loss for the perfect suggestion on etiquette, social customs, and proper decorum. He's proven himself so indispensable that I've elevated his title. No longer a mere doorman, he is now the Master of Ceremonies. Even at his young age, he's already lived more lives than one hundred men. I can't decide which life fascinates me the most, so I look forward to hearing more stories.

I lean into the mirror and powder my face. Next, I layer

some rouge on my plump cheeks and then splash my neck and wrists with a hearty dose of lilac perfume. Polly perches on my shoulder, her long elegant tail tickling my shoulder blade. I smile at her reflection and add another smudge of rouge. When Sukey moves her to the side table, I ignore her wretched screeching. Her behavior is horrible enough without encouraging it. Then Sukey teases out my black curls and pins my satin turban into place, including its towering ostrich plumes.

Thankfully the festivities don't commence until three, giving me another hour to primp. However, horses whinny and stamp their feet outside as carriage after carriage creak to a stop out front. I lose count of how many times the front door opens and shuts as eager guests arrive, flooding the entrance early.

"Why, the President's House is a perfect palace," shrieks a woman's voice as I smile to myself. More excited chatter floats up the stairs, delighting my ears.

A few minutes later, Paul stands in my doorway in his footman's livery and gives a gentle knock. "Miss Dolley, your dress is quite pretty." He shifts his feet. "It's quite early, but lots of folks are downstairs looking for you, soon as you're ready, ma'am."

I nod, smoothing my gown of rose-colored satin with its white velvet train and matching slippers. Then I bring my hand to rest on my strand of pearls.

With her mouth full of pins, Sukey shakes her head at me in the mirror, sending ripples through her tidy braids. I give her a tiniest nod. Having been pricked many times, I understand the importance of staying still.

"Thank you, Paul. I'll be down just as soon as Sukey finishes. You can start serving the refreshments now. I imagine our guests are thirsty after breathing in so much dust on their way here."

Once Sukey secures the turban to my head, I pinch my cheeks one last time and make my way down to the entrance hall, illuminated by gold lamps and lined with elegant pillars. I carry my worn copy of the popular novel, *Don Quixote,* as an easy way to start a pleasant conversation with nervous guests. Perched on my shoulder, Polly greets everyone she encounters with a shrill refrain of "Welcome to Dolley's drawing rooms." Needless to say, French John has been coaching my zany parrot for days.

Vaulted archways lead into our three drawing rooms. In the southwest corner, the palatial State Dining Room is furnished in the most elegant manner. At its head is the dramatic portrait of General Washington. I must admit Jemmy's instincts were correct after all. Hanging high on the wall, the eight-foot painting demands everyone's full attention and gives our dinner guests the opportunity to study it in depth.

With great pride, we also display smaller portraits of former Presidents Jefferson and Adams. At the center of the lengthy table lies a silver platter that illuminates our guests' faces by the gentle glow of candlelight. We splurged on fine candles made of whale blubber because they burn in an even fashion. The cheaper tallow ones sputter and reek of animal fat.

French doors open into the spacious parlor painted in my favorite shade of sunflower yellow with matching damask silk drapes and upholstered chairs. Gilbert Stuart's portrait of me hangs over the fireplace mantle. I find this rather vain, but Mr. Latrobe insisted. The small bronze clock that Abigail Adams so kindly left as a memento is on full display. This sitting room leads into the grand drawing room that we call the Elliptical Saloon.

What a sight to behold! To my great joy, Mrs. Adams would never recognize her former laundry room. The immense space now has high, cream-colored walls that high-light the magnificent oval shape with its ornate blue molding, offset by a multicolored Brussels carpet and a grand piano. Stunning artwork depicts our cherished American heroes, and picturesque country landscapes line the walls.

Crimson red curtains frame the gorgeous windows that stretch from floor to ceiling, showcasing the dramatic view of the Potomac in the distance. Much to my dismay, Mr. Latrobe believed the deep color and heavy fabric made for a terrible choice, but I splurged nonetheless. The cost was astronomical, four dollars per yard! Thankfully I'm so pleased with the result. Although I try to remain humble according to my Quaker roots, I must say the effect is truly superb.

Mr. Latrobe obtained two high-back sofas and four matching settees crafted in the popular Greek style, complete with crimson satin cushions. In addition, thirty-six black and gold Grecian chairs decorated with our national symbol sit in small semi-circles. On the marble mantle, bronze oil lamps glow, reflecting into the massive mirror edged with golden balls. The result is a shimmering light that bathes the palatial room. How I adore the magical power of this mirror here in the Elliptical Saloon.

French John is omnipresent. With great vigilance, he finds seats for tired old ladies, makes genteel introductions among strangers, and supervises the entire staff. Under his watchful eye, Sukey, Paul, and the others carry huge lacquered trays heaping with macaroons, preserves, and various cookies and cakes. Within seconds, the hungry crowd swarms in like a school of sharks and empties them. The servants also pour generous cups of coffee, Madeira wine, and Jemmy's favorite Virginia punch called a Yard of Flannel. Thank goodness it doesn't actually taste like flannel at all. It's actually a delightful mixture of ale, eggs, sugar, nutmeg and rum.

Downstairs in the kitchen, the gargantuan iron stove has

churned out steaming platters of ham, beef, crab, fish croquettes, turtle soup, and savory sweets. As a special treat, the meal will end with the delicious frozen dessert called iced creams. Mr. Jefferson enjoyed this exotic recipe in France and made it popular here in America. The servants churn it by hand for up to two hours. Then we keep it cold in our ice house using large blocks of ice cut from frozen water. Oyster is my favorite flavor, but we also offer asparagus, chestnut, and even the new popular one, pink peppermint.

When the time comes to serve it, our eager visitors consume every spoonful before a drop can melt. For those who aren't quick enough to partake, straw baskets overflow with pecans, almonds, raisins, pears, apples, and peaches. Bowls of candies wrapped in Bible verses lie on the side tables for the taking.

With poor Jemmy so small in stature, the overeager crowd pushes him about like a stable boy. Try as I might, I can't find him anywhere within the boisterous masses. Amidst the hubbub, I greet old friends by name and introduce myself to new ones with the line, "I hope you feel as at home here as I do." Since I get my energy from other people, these interactions lift me high among the clouds. Whatever help I may give to our country, I benefit just as much.

After a few minutes, though, it becomes unbearably hot. Makeup trickles down the faces of those uncouth ladies who wear it, including myself. I must say rouge and pearl powder create quite an unsightly stream when blended with sweat. Mine rolls down my face like tears, but I'm too jolly to retreat from the reception long enough to fix it. Thankfully everyone else is also full of good cheer, enjoying the delightful food and drink. To my great joy, no one can tell friend from foe within this energetic crowd. Even better, there is no mention of anyone's home state. Here and now, we're all Americans, and it's a wonderful sight to behold.

My eyes fall on my fair-haired sister Lucy chatting with widower Thomas Todd, the handsome Supreme Court Justice from Kentucky. She's smiling, a rare occurrence since her heartbreak as a young widow. Now she is actually laughing, which warms my heart! Ah, this is the fun-loving sister I've so sorely missed. Watching her enjoy herself, even for a few minutes, makes this gathering a roaring success in my eyes, and well worth the weeks of preparation. In her comical way, she flails her arms to flag me down. "We've enjoyed some tasty drinks. Would you share a little snuff with us?"

Of course, I open my bejeweled silver box, only too happy to oblige her. "Here you are, my silly one!" Then I whisper in her ear, "Sister, I love to see you joyful. I pray you find love again as I did with Jemmy."

She clutches my arm as I greet our esteemed guest. "Justice Todd, how wonderful to see you again. What an honor to have you here with us today."

"Why, thank you, Mrs. Madison. Your drawing rooms are enchanting, but I find your sister even more so."

Raising her hand to her forehead, Lucy pretends to swoon and quips, "I can see the snuff is already affecting your good judgement."

Unfortunately, my euphoria over my sister's glorious transformation into her former bubbly self is short-lived. As I stroll through the rooms making niceties, I cannot help but overhear the wife of a Federalist Congressman hiss to her companion, "Just look at Madison standing over there alone. What a grumpy sourpuss he is!" Despite the lively conversation and delightful music from both our new piano and a guitar, her stage whisper carries like a shout. Her cruel comment about my darling husband stops me in my tracks.

To my dismay, this loathsome woman swills down some whiskey punch and persists in ridiculing him some more. "That gloomy stiff creature has nothing engaging or even bearable in his manners. He's the most unsociable creature in existence. I'm convinced that he's incapable of smiling. I bet she married him just for all the attention she'd get. Why else would she want to spend the rest of her life with him?"

Batting my eyes, I feign ignorance and murmur the friendliest welcome I can muster. "Victoria honey, how wonderful to have you join my dear Jemmy and me this afternoon. I was so thrilled when he appointed your husband to the Committee on Elections. I'm sure he'll become quite a valuable member."

As I proceed onward, I glance back into the gilded mirror which reveals her blushing as red as my new drapes. While her nasty remarks sting like an angry hornet, her opinion makes no difference to me. Not knowing the real Jemmy is a loss for her. He's kind to a fault, even to vulgar people like her. Plus, he works harder than anyone in the country and perhaps the entire world.

Alas, I wish those were the only hateful comments, but they ripple through the crowd and drift into my pained ears. Of course, I choose to ignore them all, holding my head a bit higher and plastering on an angelic smile as the barbs continue.

"Poor Little Jemmy, he's but a shriveled little apple."

"Yes, what an old, sour-eyed man. There's no dash of youth in him."

"I agree. He's got one foot in the grave!"

"He looks like a schoolmaster dressed for a funeral."

I must admit there's some truth to this last one. For years, I've begged him to wear a suit in another color or perhaps long pants, the latest fashion for men, but to no avail.

Next in my path, I'm delighted to encounter the outgoing James Monroe, Jemmy's new Secretary of State. "Mrs. Madison, what a spectacular gathering." He scans the room with wide eyes. "Your new drawing rooms are absolutely marvelous. I am amazed by what you've done here."

Monroe is almost six feet tall, and he wears the old-style knee britches and buckled shoes like Jemmy. With his high forehead and wide blue-gray eyes, he is a dignified fellow Virginian. As I embrace his huge frame, I avoid his left shoulder which still bears a musket ball from the Revolution.

In the past he's been both a friend and rival. Years ago, he ran against Jemmy for the First Congress, but Jemmy prevailed. Then just recently, he challenged Jemmy for the presidency at Randolph's urging. We are grateful that friction is now behind us and pray our good relations will continue. His stunning wife, Elizabeth, and I greet each other as well. Her empire dress with its high waist flaunts her exquisite figure, jet black hair, and blue eyes.

Across the crowded room, I spy the dreadful Congressman Randolph. He has spoken horrible untruths of Jemmy and me on many occasions, even calling Jemmy a pole-cat, which is a fancy word for a skunk. He may be Tom's cousin, but he is no Virginia gentleman in my opinion. Even worse, he uses his nasty tongue to oppose the war at every opportunity. Nonetheless, I feign delight at his company and inquire about his family with all the politeness I can manage. We must placate him as best we can. He gestures to my distant cousin, Francis Scott Key, a reputable lawyer from Georgetown.

"It's such a pleasure to see you again, Mr. Key." Truly it is. I never tire of visiting with my relatives, even if he is a crony of Randolph. He too is a vocal opponent of the war, declaring it an abominable lump of wickedness. However, my goal is to defray those bitter feelings between us Republicans and the Federalists, even within my own family. In my mind, such healing starts with genuine kindness toward each other.

Thankfully, a true friend stands in my path, Speaker Clay.

His eyes sparkle like a peacock displaying its dazzling array of feathers.

"Mrs. Madison, I admire your work here. I'll admit that I was skeptical at first, but it's absolutely stunning. In fact, I hardly recognize the place."

"Thank you so much, Mr. Speaker. I'm proud to say that Mr. Latrobe and I accomplished our goals but still came in under your budget." I wink. "Take that lesson to Congress to change their spendthrift ways."

He laughs as I open my bejeweled box and offer him some snuff. "Why certainly, Madam. How could I refuse? After all, everybody loves Mrs. Madison." He gathers some powdered tobacco and inhales it. I partake as well, using a lace handkerchief to hide my stained one underneath.

"That's because Mrs. Madison loves everybody," I reply with a sly smile, my cheeks warm. I credit my upbringing for teaching me to find the good in everyone. However, some people are much harder to love than others.

As if to prove my point, Rosalie Calvert's Belgian accent floats into my ear. "I have come here to pay court to Queen Dolla Lolla. I see even her snuffbox has a magical influence on men, everyone but her husband," she scoffs. "After all, he is so weak and ineffective. But then again, anyone is better than that wretched Tommy Jeff." To my frustration, Rosalie insists on badmouthing us, despite my unfailing kindness to her.

Of course, I pretend not to hear. Instead, I remind myself of the huge distance that separates her from her extended family, which must be difficult to bear. My heart would break if the vast Atlantic Ocean kept me from my two dear sisters for years on end.

"Bah! I'm not impressed. This is far from the royal levées that I've attended in Europe." She sniffs and runs her hand along the door, rolling her eyes. "This wood is only painted

pine. At Riversdale, ours are all made of rich mahogany."
Then she turns to Mr. Key. "On your return home, please tell
your wife that she missed nothing of importance here. Of
course, I do send her my best."

As usual, I decide to rise above her antics. With my
cheeks aflame, I look for Jemmy, wondering who he'd like me
to escort over to him. I take a sweeping glance across the
room—filled with diplomats, government officials, and
laborers in greasy boots. To my delight, it is a true mix of
people enjoying each other's company.

"You have such a gift for bringing people together."
Margaret hugs me and then links her arm through mine.
"Your husband is brilliant, but hospitality is the presiding
genius of this house."

"You are too kind, my friend." I reply, giving her elbow a
squeeze. "Many thanks to you for posting the notice in the
paper."

"Well, after your great success today, we certainly won't
need to advertise again." She beams at me. "The word will
spread like the city has been set on fire."

From the corner of my eye, I finally spot Jemmy lurking in
the shadows against the wall. He's engrossed in conversation
with Congressman John C. Calhoun, the young War Hawk
from South Carolina whose long gray locks hang like a lion's
mane. Mr. Calhoun towers over Jemmy, ranting about
evicting the British from Canada. Jemmy listens with a
furrowed brow as he rocks on his heels.

Then the brazen Congressman Daniel Webster waltzes up
to Jemmy with a sneer. "So, here's the little occupant of the
great White House."

My unflappable husband doesn't react to the Federalist
leader, but Calhoun bristles with such force that his mane
shakes, too. Thankfully he doesn't emit a roar as well.

I flag down Sukey and tell her to deliver some seed cake

and punch to them right away. Delicious food works wonders in tense situations—in any situation, really. This is contrary to the Quaker belief that the purpose of food is provide only nourishment, not pleasure. In the meantime, I meander over to greet Mr. Webster and inquire about his family in New Hampshire.

CHAPTER 9
EVERYONE SQUEEZES IN
MAY 1809

The end of our official invitation to receive guests is five o'clock. However, the festivities continue until midnight since no one bothers to look at the time, especially me. Male admirers swarm around my friend Betsy Bonaparte, almost blocking her from view. As the hours fly by, many well-dressed ladies focus their energy on staring at her, their jaws slack, as they gossip back and forth. "Why, the men flock to her more than the whiskey punch!" exclaims one woman wearing an outdated hoop skirt. In addition to her disapproval, I detect a distinct note of jealousy.

"It's because all the clothes she wears could fit into my pocket," replies her friend in a snooty voice. The others toss their heads and leave the area in a huff, whispering amongst themselves.

"*Oui*, I must agree." Next to me, Rosalie Calvert rolls her eyes. "Her dress is quite see-through and much too tight. And she wears no chemise underneath at all. Heavens, you can even see her skin and the shape of her thigh. She's almost naked!" She points her nose in the air. "And she has the nerve to wonder why the Emperor Napoleon didn't accept her into the House of Bonaparte?"

I look around the room, making sure everyone is engaged in a good chat. People of all kinds interest me, but spreading rumors about them does not. One of the sources of my happiness is having no desire to know the business of others.

Desperate to get away, I stroll over to Margaret who announces, "I'm highly pleased with the becoming spirit of these ladies. Next time Betsy must promise to wear more clothes." She crosses her arms and looks me in the eye. "You really must tell her to dress differently or no one will invite her anymore."

I want to point out the dense circle of men begging to accompany her anywhere, but I bite my lip instead. Poor Betsy has no idea she's the frequent subject of such malicious talk. Somehow, I must remove the thorn from this precarious situation. Otherwise, these busybodies may spark the first female duel in history at my drawing rooms. Wouldn't I become the laughing stock then? Jemmy would tease me for years.

"Honey," I call over to Betsy, wedging myself among her hopeful suitors. Eventually I work my way over to her and pat her arm. "I've sent Sukey off to fetch me a shawl. Would you care for one as well?"

"Oh, Dolley, that would be lovely." She leans into me. "There's a bit of a chill in the air. You're such a dear friend."

Ah, another crisis averted by a simple act of kindness. Imagine what this world could achieve if we united forces in good cheer and civility. How I despise arguing with people, no matter how much we disagree. If it comes right down to it, I'd rather fight with my hands than my tongue, even with my Quaker roots as a pacifist.

In the distance, I spy a lanky young man from the back-woods. He stands alone, pressed against the back wall. I don't know his name, but I do recall meeting his mother years ago. Once half an hour passes with him still in that awkward position, I fret over how to help him without adding to his discomfort. I love nothing better than putting people at ease.

So, I send Sukey over near him to hand out coffee, and he ventures forward to receive a cup. I take that opportunity to greet him. He startles at the sight of me, spilling his drink as the saucer falls onto the rug. Then he jams the dripping cup into his pocket.

"My apologies, the crowd is so great." I reach out and touch his shoulder. "No one can avoid being jostled, including me. I'll have my servant bring you another cup right away."

He stares at me, unable to utter a word.

"Pray, how is your excellent mother?" I ask him in a subdued tone. "I had the opportunity to meet her once, but it has been quite a while now, I'm afraid."

"She's quite well, thank you, Mrs. Madison." His drawn face brightens into a smile. "She still speaks so fondly of meeting you."

"I hope we shall see each other again soon, but please do give her my best regards." As I saunter away, he pulls the cup from his pocket and slides it onto the nearest table.

※

MY DRAWING ROOMS CONTINUE EVERY WEDNESDAY afternoon, each attracting more partygoers than the last. As the sweltering heat of summer sets in, I douse myself with even more lilac perfume and throw open all the windows. I receive everyone, no matter how unpleasant their political views. After all, this is truly the fulfillment of my dream. Political enemies enter our home and engage in polite conversations. As a result, we get to know each other as people.

Then we can exchange ideas that will develop into policies to advance our country.

No matter how large the masses, everyone manages to squeeze, crush, or jam themselves inside. Nowadays my gatherings are referred to as "squeezes," a nickname which warms my heart. Although I'm thrilled, presiding over these packed rooms sometimes overwhelms even me. The attention can make me dizzy, but I don't let on to anyone, especially my beloved husband.

CHAPTER 10
OUR FIRST STATE DINNER

LATE 1809

S ince my squeezes have created such a sensation, I embark upon another tradition—gathering political wives in my cozy parlor for coffee. Of course, I also serve hot bouillon and warm sardine tea toasts to rejuvenate everyone as they come inside from the frigid temperatures. Then we enjoy some soft gingerbread from Mr. Jefferson's favorite recipe and discuss the looming prospect of a second war with Great Britain.

I use this opportunity to explain Jemmy's views. My plan is to sway them, so they will go home and convince their husbands. While they're here, I also request their favorite dinner recipes. When they finally trickle out the door one-by-one, I wave them off with a sad smile. I already look forward to our next get-together which I shall call a Dove Party.

Searching for company, I deliver a steaming cup of coffee to Jemmy in his office along with some leftover slices of cake. I put the tray on his desk, pretending it is all for him, but we both know the truth. The coffee is for him, and the cake is for me.

He looks up from his huge stack of correspondence, takes a sip of coffee, and flips over to the next letter. "How was the gathering? You ladies sounded rather lively down there. Quite a racket, even without Polly joining in."

"It was great fun, so I've decided to make it a regular event." Then I broach a new subject. "Jemmy, don't you think we should hold a State Dinner soon? That would make another fine American tradition."

"You know me, I'm in no hurry to add such frivolous things. I have more work than I have time for as it is." He gestures to the pile. "Just look at this little mountain." He puts on a whimsical look. "Perhaps I should call it my own 'Monticello' since that's the Italian translation."

"Well, the real Monticello is far lovelier." I pull my chair up to the desk and nibble on some cake. "Why don't we try one State Dinner and see how you like it. Who knows? You might even enjoy yourself!"

He shakes his head. "President Jefferson made many social blunders at his dinners that I don't care to repeat." He takes another sip and glances down, eager to get back to his work.

"Yes, I am well aware of that, especially since one of them involved me." I sigh and indulge myself in a bit more cake. "I still can't believe he insisted on escorting me into dinner instead of the British Minister's wife." I wave my hands, trying to make those unpleasant memories disappear. "But this will be entirely different. I have a plan."

"I'm sure you do, my darling. Just give me my marching orders." He gives me a mock salute and leans back in his chair, stretching out his arms behind him.

"Well, the French Minister will be in town next month, so I propose we do it then." Raising my fork like I'm toasting, I take another generous bite. "Since he's so revolting, having a large group will make the interaction much easier. Plus, that will give his wife more of a chance to mingle. I shudder to think of what it's like for poor Marguerite being married to him."

General Louis-Marie Turreau de Garambonville is well-known as a scoundrel in Washington City. In addition to his long name, he has had a lengthy career. He is a veteran of both our Revolution as well as the French Revolution. More recently, while serving as Napoleon's General, he became infamous for massacring tens of thousands of innocent people as he ravaged the European countryside.

"Agreed. They do call him the Lizard after all." He leans forward. "But here's the part that worries me. Whom shall I escort into dinner? You or Marguerite?"

"Neither!" I give him a dazzling smile as I finish off the slice.

"No one?" His eyes widen. "Really?"

"Yes, really! We will revert to traditional etiquette. Unlike the days of Mr. Jefferson, our guests will not rush into the dining room pell-mell style and choose their own seats. I will assign each person to a specific chair."

"Go on." Jemmy nods.

"Then the Marine Corps Band will play a new song called 'Hail to the Chief' as you march into the room. 'Hail, Columbia' will come next since it's our unofficial national anthem."

"This sounds too formal and a bit pompous for my taste." His face tightens.

"You're so humble, but consider this, Jemmy." I raise a finger. "A grand entrance would allow our guests to reflect on your important role as our commander in chief."

"I understand, but I'm still not entirely convinced." He clears his throat.

"With war looming on the horizon, we need to bolster your image as a strong leader. America also needs to develop its customs. In order for us to thrive, the presidency must receive our utmost respect. Hopefully this will become the standard for future presidents as well. It's intimidating to launch a new tradition, but each must begin with a first. I pray this one will endure."

"All right, my dear. After all, I trust your instincts better than my own in these matters. Let's try it."

"Wonderful. And there's one more thing. I do propose one definite breach of etiquette."

"How so?" He cocks his head.

"I'd like to sit at the head of the table and have you in the middle amongst our guests."

"Why is that?" Jemmy pinches his eyebrows together.

"Well, you prefer talking to people directly rather than addressing a group. And this way you'll be at the center of the conversation. As we both know, these dinner discussions often lead to important deals and decisions."

"Hmm, you do have a point there." He rubs his chin and reflects for a moment. "Perhaps that would work out nicely."

THE EVENING OF OUR FIRST STATE DINNER SOON ARRIVES. Right on the appointed hour, our guest of honor arrives in his glittering golden carriage. Jemmy and I stand in the doorway and gape at this vision of extravagance, a stark contrast to the ocean of mud surrounding our home. The slim figure of the French Minister emerges, dripping with lace and gold and a firm grip on the elbow of my friend, Marguerite. Despite her breathtaking pastel gown that brings out her green eyes, the lines in her exquisite face betray her deep unhappiness. Her husband is also well known for mistreating this darling woman who teaches me about French fashion with such kindness.

In addition, we welcome thirty other esteemed guests

with crystal goblets of exquisite French wine and Polly perched on my shoulder. With great care, I curated an impressive list of American dignitaries and local Francophiles. Of course, I included many members of the Cabinet, Congress, and the Supreme Court, including the influential Chief Justice, John Marshall, despite the fact that he is Federalist.

When Betsy Bonaparte enters the oval saloon, French John formally announces her arrival. The French Minister's eyes rove up and down her revealing gown. "Mademoiselle Patterson, how enchanting to see you," he sneers. "I have heard so much."

"As you are well aware, my name is Madame Bonaparte." Her eyes narrow, and she takes a step back.

"Not according to the Emperor Napoleon, Mademoiselle Patterson." He raises an eyebrow at her.

With a sudden flapping of her long wings, Polly lets out a blood-curdling screech.

"Hush!" I snap at her.

Undeterred by my scolding, she dive-bombs at the ogling French Minister. "No, Polly, no!" I scream.

Thankfully Jemmy reaches his hand into the air and intercepts her. We certainly don't need Polly straining our crucial relations with France. After all, Margaret and her husband are here with the *National Intelligencer*, writing a story about this historic event.

Frustrated, Polly bites down on Jemmy's index finger with a resounding crunch. He winces as the crowd lets out a collective gasp. To my relief, Polly soars off in a huff to sulk in her cage. French John trots along behind her to secure it for the evening.

"It's my second battle scar in the service of our country." Jemmy musters a wan smile and looks over at Monroe. "The first happened back when we ran against each other for the

First Congress. I got frostbite on my nose." He tilts his head. "As you can see, I've still got the ugly scar to prove it, but I've never been known for my fine looks."

Paul and Sukey rush over to tend to Jemmy. As they escort him from the room, he forces a laugh and waves his uninjured hand to the shocked group.

"Ignore that hateful man," I whisper in Betsy's ear. Then I grab her hand and pull her away from that cretin amidst the confusion. Then I make an announcement, asking our guests to find their seats.

I make sure to seat the French Minister and Marguerite directly across from Jemmy. How I would love to whisk Marguerite away and have her near me. However, even I don't dare make such an unusual arrangement. I place the ambitious Speaker Clay and his wife, Lucretia, on Jemmy's right. After all, Clay is known as the Rising Star of the West. The likable Secretary of State Monroe and Elizabeth sit to Jemmy's left. My cousin, Edmund Coles, sits at the foot of the table as Jemmy's secretary, taking a flurry of notes for Jemmy to review tomorrow morning.

Always a matchmaker, I make sure to put Lucy alongside Justice Todd. The dazzling glow on her face is a sight to behold. He's called on her several times already and made his serious intentions known. They whisper back and forth, not even glancing at my sister Anna and her husband Richard across from them, much to their amusement.

Within a few minutes, Jemmy enters the dining room with a bandaged finger and heads straight for his chair. However, I escort him back out, ensuring that he make a dignified entrance despite the rather awkward circumstances. Our feisty parrot will not sideline President James Madison.

"As you wish, Queen Dolley," he mutters.

"Everyone, please stand," I command the group.

The Marine Corps Band plays 'Hail to the Chief' as

instructed, and our president marches in to great clapping and cheering. When they follow with 'Hail, Columbia,' Jemmy slides into his chair with a genuine smile. I am now even more confident in my decision.

Presiding over the guests, I lead them in a light-hearted conversation, trying to include every esteemed guest. After a few minutes, I raise my wine glass in a toast. "To excellent future relations with our cherished French friends, far and wide."

Then I turn to John Quincy Adams and Louisa seated by me. "And to our new Ambassador to Russia and his lovely wife. We are honored to have you both represent us and wish you wonderful adventures abroad!"

"My congratulations to you, Louisa," says Betsy across the table. "I admire your strength with your boys. I don't know if I could make such a sacrifice. Short trips abroad are wonderful of course, but not for years. At least you'll have baby Charles to keep you company during those long Russian winters."

"What do you mean?" Stunned, Louisa blinks back at her and puts her glass down. "I don't understand. Our whole family is going."

"Please forgive me." Betsy blushes to the roots of her hair, quite a contrast to her ivory complexion. "I thought your older boys are going to stay here. Obviously I must have misunderstood. My sincere apologies."

"What are you saying?" Poor Louisa's eyes well up with tears. "No one has consulted me about such a proposal." The blood drains from her face as if she's been struck with a blow. She turns to John Quincy and stares at him, open-mouthed.

"It's in the boys' best interest, Louisa," he murmurs. "We will discuss it later." He stares down at the French lace table-cloth, avoiding her teary glare.

Reaching over, I pat Louisa on the back but don't say a

word. I am crushed for her. How could her husband fail to consult her on such a major decision? Alas, it's none of my business, though. My only way to help is by smoothing it over as best I can. For now, that means changing the subject and adjusting everyone's focus onto another guest while the devastated Louisa collects herself. No stranger to public humiliation, Betsy looks equally miserable for broaching this sensitive topic and causing such anguish.

I ensured that we used local foods to prepare the recipes shared by the political wives. After all, our table represents America's table. For the bountiful main course, I use my new Loughstaff China edged in blue and gold. After a bowl of Macaroni Soup a la Napeoliatine, I serve oysters, turtle, and saltwater fish with potato rolls called Madison Cakes. Fairy butter is one of my favorite concoctions, so I make sure to include this delicious blend of hard-boiled eggs, orange-flower water, powdered sugar, and butter.

"I can practically hear the table groaning under this abundance of dishes," quips Speaker Clay. "Mrs. Madison, you have outdone yourself once again."

When I start to carve an assortment of wild game with deer, turkey, and duck, Vice President Clinton jumps to his feet despite his ill health. "Please may I assist you, Mrs. Madison?"

"Thank you so much, Mr. Vice President. You are so kind to offer, but I do this quite regularly. Please watch with what ease I do it."

"Ah, bon." The French Minister curls his lip and taunts me, "It is as if you were born and educated at Versailles."

I muster a demure smile, quite aware he is mocking me. It is no secret that I lack any formal schooling and do not speak French. Moreover, no member of French Royalty would ever deign to carve a roast.

"Bah! This is more like a farmer's harvest home supper," scoffs Rosalie Calvert in a hushed tone meant to carry.

When the French Minister reaches past Marguerite to pour himself yet another glass of wine, she flinches. I pray no one else has noticed. Without a doubt, though, the intense candlelight reveals a patchwork of finger-shaped bruises around my friend's neck. Her attempt to camouflage them with powder has been futile; they are far too dark to hide.

Without a hint of awkwardness, Jemmy launches into several whimsical stories that include hilarious rhymes. Soon we all roar so hard that we gasp for breath. After all, there is no better storyteller than my Jemmy when he is relaxed among friends.

Next, we enjoy a sumptuous dessert of apricot iced creams, macaroons, preserves, and my favorite layer cake frosted with caramel. Just as our stomachs are bursting with this fine food, the servants set out a second dessert. There's a dazzling assortment of almonds, pecans, raisins, apples, and pears. Afterward we play parlor games, sing along to the piano, and some even dance.

While Jemmy escorts the last Congressman to the door, Sukey and I gather up the remaining dishes from the Elliptical Saloon. I hum under my breath, elated by the evening's success. When the door finally shuts with a resounding thud, Jemmy lets out an uncharacteristic whoop, startling me so much that I nearly drop my armful of plates.

Whirling around, I stare at my husband as he rushes back into the room. All of a sudden, I'm worried. Perhaps his finger had him in severe pain all night, and he found the interactions insufferable. If that is the case, though, he put on a great show of pretending to enjoy himself.

To my surprise, he reaches up and kisses me on the cheek. "Dearest, you're even more brilliant than I ever imagined.

Why, I got more work done over that dinner than I did all last week, chained to my desk."

Then he holds up his wounded finger with a grin. "And that naughty girl of ours did us a favor by going after the Lizard, something we all wanted to do."

I burst out laughing and wrap my arms around him.

"So, when can we have our next State Dinner?" he asks, pressed against my neck. "Tomorrow night?"

"Perhaps not quite so soon, Mr. President." I pull back and beam at him. "But I'm thrilled you found it productive. I'll plan one soon enough, don't worry. In the meantime, our next event will be on New Year's Day. We'll continue Mr. Jefferson's lovely tradition of opening the President's House to visitors."

๛

INDEED, ON THE FIRST OF JANUARY, WE PREPARE TO HOST A large gathering from noon to one o'clock. Much to my delight, though, a fabulous gala is underway well before the grandfather clock strikes the hour. The Marine Band plays with its usual fervor in the entrance area despite the lively guests pressing against their heads.

Ignoring the frigid weather, I choose a yellow silk dress embroidered with delicate flowers and butterflies. No two are alike, and they change color with the light. It reminds me of the balmy spring weather we all crave right now. Thankfully the thick crowd and roaring blazes in every fireplace keep me warm. Since I'm inside, I needn't worry about the frozen mud and frustrating poor Sukey with the impossible task of removing a smattering of brown stains.

CHAPTER 11
WAR FEVER
APRIL 1812

To my great delight, April starts off on a wonderful note with sunny skies for the first Easter Egg Roll. Thomas, our new gardener, has achieved a small miracle by growing some grass in the front yard, eliminating a substantial portion of the muck. Ah, we have come so far from the days of Mr. Jefferson's roaming sheep and his two caged grizzly bears from the explorer Zebulon Pike. Sukey and I take over the kitchen, boiling a mountain of eggs with red flannel, turning them all scarlet.

Under my supervision, hundreds of children gather here to race on the lawn with long wooden spoons. Of course, my dear nephews and niece are part of the group. As the competition begins, they all set off in a tizzy, pushing their crimson eggs toward the finish line. The sound of their high-pitched squeals is well worth my efforts.

Jemmy and I cheer as our oldest nephew, James Madison Cutts, elbows his younger brother out of the way and charges first across the finish line. Ignoring his wailing brother, he waves his spoon over his head and bellows, "Victory is mine!"

"There's no shyness about him, is there?" Jemmy asks, his blue eyes twinkling.

❦

UNFORTUNATELY, OUR JOVIAL MOOD DOESN'T LAST LONG. The sickly Vice President George Clinton soon perishes from a heart attack on April 20. However, with the dreaded election looming ahead in November, Jemmy decides to leave the slot vacant.

The War Hawks continue to pound their steady drumbeat for war. Heated debates rage daily in Congress, and they last for hours on end. My friends and I have been flocking there for months, drawn like mosquitos to a fresh mud puddle.

As Sukey finishes securing the turban that matches my new gown, I announce to Jemmy, "Hannah Gallatin and I are off to Congress again today. Every day is a whole new performance. It's so entertaining, like going to a show."

"It certainly is, my dear. It's the best show in town. I have piles of correspondence to wade through, but I look forward to hearing your stories tonight."

"With Lucy gone, I'm thankful for any distraction." My eyes fill with tears as I splash myself with lilac perfume. "Having her wedding here in the Elliptical Saloon was so lovely. I'm delighted for her new life with Justice Todd in Kentucky, but my heart still aches at losing her. Her letters just aren't enough, even though one arrives every day."

"I know how you miss her, my dearest." He gives me a peck on the forehead. "It is bittersweet indeed."

"Lucy was only teasing when she said Anna could only try to fill her void." I shake my head and then put on my rouge. "But she was spot on."

"I do miss laughing with her." He smiles, reminiscing.

76

"She's more refreshing than a long walk. No one can play a bit of a fool like Lucy."

"Well, at least Justice Todd has to come to Washington City for two months out of every year for court. Of course, I made him promise to bring her along." I lean into the mirror and put on my lipstick.

"Now there's something to look forward to, my dear. Without her here, though, Congress offers the only entertainment in this tiny town. That's other than your squeezes, of course."

"Yes, but the theatrics at Congress are better than London's Theatre Royal. Hopefully our feminine presence will prevent an outright duel between Speaker Clay and Randolph."

"We can only hope." Jemmy chuckles. "But if it doesn't, please make sure to step out of the way. Their deep animosity guarantees a bloody mess."

"I will be sure not to stain my new gown. After all, it came at quite a price." I grab my shawl and tie it around my shoulders.

"Don't they all, my darling?" He raises an eyebrow.

With Paul driving, I collect Hannah and head to the Capitol. She and I lift our long skirts and shuffle down the wobbly planks to the Hall of Representatives. As we proceed through the arched entrances into the chamber, the fluted Corinthian columns carved by Italian sculptors take my breath away, just as they do every time. Our lady friends wave us over to the seats they saved for us in the packed gallery.

In the midst of a stormy address railing against British tyranny, Speaker Clay stops himself mid-sentence. He greets us with a wide smile and a magnanimous bow. "Welcome to the Presidentess and Mrs. Gallatin as well. We are honored to add such esteemed guests to our spectators. What an especially beautiful group of ladies we have gathered here today."

We all titter. I have yet to encounter a woman who is immune to his charms.

Within an instant, though, Speaker Clay returns to his podium surrounded by crimson silk curtains. Looming large behind him is an oversized marble statue of a seated Lady Liberty. A carved American bald eagle with a twelve-foot wingspan stands by her side. He resumes skewering the Federalists who oppose the war, gesturing with his long arms. His voice sounds like a pipe organ, and his hair waves to a beat of its own. It's a masterpiece of oratory and theater. Even those who vehemently disagree with him are cast under his spell.

"What kind of nation allows its enemy to kidnap its sailors and force them into their navy for years?" he thunders. "What point was the War of Independence if we are just going to roll over and give into these bullies and tyrants? Our most valuable treasure is our honor. Without it, what do we have left?"

He pounds on the podium. "Nothing, I tell you! How can we live with ourselves if we continue to let Britain steal our sailors, take our ships, and encourage the Indians on the western frontier to shoot us? They even supply them with weapons. Our flag means nothing to them. We must stand up for our nation now before it's too late!"

Congressman Daniel Webster shoots his hand into the air and trots up to the front. "The Federal Government hasn't raised any money to pay for this war of yours, Mr. Speaker. May also I remind you that we no longer have a National Bank? This is economic suicide, not to mention foolhardy and self-destructive. Britain is our biggest trading partner and still the world's mightiest empire."

He leans over the podium and shakes his finger at the entire group. "To the War Hawks out there calling for war, hear me now! You boys are as immature as our country. You didn't suffer through the Revolution. You weren't even alive for the Declaration of Independence. Do you realize the few soldiers we have are ancient holdovers from decades ago? We have seventeen ships; they have over 1,000. We have 12,000 soldiers; they have 250,000. Exactly what kind of lunacy are you proposing? Do you think this self-sabotage is really worth it just to soothe our injured national pride?"

Ignoring the thunderous applause by the Federalists, Congressman John C. Calhoun strides up to the podium next. He stares down the unruly crowd, person by person, until silence reigns. "Gentlemen, impressment is kidnapping. They've been plundering our ships on the high seas for five years and snatched 5,000 American sailors against their will." He thumps his fist. "We can't stand for this outrageous piracy one moment longer. Our embargoes have done nothing but hurt our own economy. Enough! It's high time to standup to those brutes!"

I summon all my self-control to keep myself from applauding. Once again, he has earned his nickname, Hercules.

To no one's surprise, the abrasive Congressman Randolph won't let this rest. I hold my breath as he swaggers to the podium on his stilt-like legs. At first glance, he looks like a sickly boy with a handkerchief tied around his head. Strangely enough, though, wrinkles cover his face, and his hair is gray. As usual, he has his pack of ornery hunting dogs in tow, snarling just like their master. Wearing spurred boots, he cracks a riding whip like he's closing in on a kill.

My jaw drops as he chugs down a bottle of ale. His outrageous conduct never fails to horrify me.

"Sergeant at Arms, remove those animals from this chamber at once!" shouts Speaker Clay as he bangs the gavel.

"One beast in here is enough!" mutters Hannah as a shocked stillness takes hold.

"Even that's too much for my taste," I whisper, choking back a guffaw.

"He fancies himself a Member of Parliament," she murmurs back.

"He's even too strange for that." I stifle my laughter, pretending to sneeze into my kerchief as Randolph's strange soprano voice fills the packed room. Like Clay and Webster, he is a brilliant speaker, but his style is flashier and comes peppered with inflammatory remarks.

"This warmongering is madness and sponsored by ignorant fools," he declares. "It's like going to war against our brother. Let's not forget how much we owe England. We share the same language, religion, legal system, representative government, and even Shakespeare and Newton."

The odd yet eloquent Randolph extends his rant, making no effort to control his fury. "The barren rocks of Bermuda are worth more than Canada." He glares around the room, shaking his finger like a club. "Mark my words, nature will prove to be our greatest enemy in this war. Think of the roads, the transportation, and the weather. Do you even realize how mammoth our country is now with the Louisiana Territory? It's larger than all of Europe. Heed my warning. This war will be financed by the blood and treasure of our people."

With his sharp temper on full display, he hisses at his fellow Congressmen, "It's greed that urges this war. We've only heard a single word repeated like the whippoorwill's monotonous call, 'Canada! Canada! Canada!' All else is whitewash."

"Enough!" Speaker Clay retorts. "Canada is rich in natural resources—wood, fish, and fur, not to mention a vast expanse of land. I firmly believe they want us to annex them. Why wouldn't they want to shake off their British oppressors just like we did? I will be the first to declare that this war will end with Canada at our feet! In fact, I predict they will even welcome us with cheers at the border."

He continues, "Remember, their land up north is almost five times bigger than the Louisiana Purchase, and the Brits don't have many troops there to defend it. They're all consumed with fighting Napoleon. We'd be fools not to grab their colony while we can. It's there for the taking. Free Canada! And let's kick the Brits off our continent once and for all. We must prevent them from ever invading us from the north!"

With a mighty slam of the gavel, Speaker Clay adjourns the session. The crowd files out as a miserable silence hangs heavy over the room. This unrelenting strife has my insides going topsy-turvy, but I link arms with Hannah. Holding my head up high, I force myself to focus on my brand-new dress from Paris. I must appear confident although I feel anything but that.

However, one thing is certain. The United States are not united at all.

CHAPTER 12
WE DECLARE WAR
JUNE 18, 1812

By June of 1812, my pragmatic husband makes the boldest decision of his life. He finally takes action, drafting a formal declaration of war. Even after exhausting every diplomatic option available, the Brits still refuse to stop abusing our countrymen. They have been relentless for years, trying to reduce us to their obedient Colonists once again. We are woefully unprepared for such a tremendous military action, but so be it.

From the packed gallery, my gaggle of friends and I listen to each speaker with rapt attention. "Let war be proclaimed against England," Speaker Clay roars. "There can be no motive for delay. Any further discussion, any new attempt at negotiation, would be as fruitless as it would be dishonorable." I want to stand up and cheer, but that is far from ladylike.

The Senate votes in favor, 19-13, as well as the House, 79-49. However, it is quite a narrow margin for such a momentous decision. Of course, the Federalists remain unanimous in their opposition with none voting in favor. I'm not sure whether to be happy, but today we are making history. After all, this is the first time for America to declare war on another country during its short existence.

As we join the massive crowd exiting the room, Randolph races back to the podium and issues a scathing rebuke to our backs. Naturally he minces no words. "Gentlemen, you have made war! Mark my words, this will lead to the ruin of our country. Before you can capture Canada, your idol Napoleon will no longer be a distraction for the world, and our Capitol will be in ruins. We are far too inexperienced for this venture."

Despite the oppressive heat, a shiver runs down my spine. Of course, I hide my anxious soul and appear merry.

As everyone pours out of the Senate vestibule onto the street, both friends and foe swarm around Jemmy and me, vying for our attention. Jemmy wears a round black hat with a red, white and blue cockade as well as a rose-shaped badge, designating himself as our commander in chief. Thankfully it adds to his height, so I can track his slight frame in the surging crowd that separates us.

In the midst of the commotion out front, a woman in a carriage stands up and loosens her bun. Then she pulls each comb from her head, one by one. Eventually her hair flows down to her knees. "Hear me now!" she shrieks. "I will part with it all and use it to hang Madison!" She holds up some scissors and cuts her long locks to her scalp as we horrified onlookers give a collective gasp. Oh, even I shall find it hard to forgive that. Decency has departed from this fallen world.

"What a horror," my husband mutters as we jump into our carriage and escape the dramatic scene.

"Oh, she's just a lunatic, Jemmy. Don't give her a second thought."

"That woman back there? I hardly noticed her." He shrugs. "Unfortunately, we have far bigger problems than that. America is now at war, and I'm at the helm."

We stare at each other, stupefied.

"How in the world has this come to pass?" he finally sputters. "I'm a friend of peace, and I want nothing more than to maintain it. Yet I just launched our fragile country into war against the greatest power on Earth. I've never taken such a dangerous action."

"But Jemmy, you had no choice! They've trampled all over us for years." My voice shakes as I feel my face flush. "You tried everything—diplomacy, embargoes, and never-ending negotiations. They all failed miserably, every single one. Those brutes still bully us to this day and will keep doing so until we force them to stop."

"No matter how necessary an evil, this is still a terrible way to start a war." He wrinkles his nose. "We have no real standing army. Jefferson and I insisted on that years ago, contrary to Hamilton's plan, because we feared a dictatorship. Ah, what naïve fools we were."

I want to offer words of comfort, but none come to mind.

"I've already called up the state militias, but the New Englanders refuse to send theirs." He frowns and throws his hands in the air. "And I can't do anything about it. The Treasury is almost bankrupt, but Jefferson and I also led the opposition to the National Bank." He puts his palms together and looks upward. "Dear God in Heaven, I hope this will be as simple as the War Hawks so firmly believe."

"Amen," I whisper.

"This is the riskiest thing I've ever done, even more than the Constitution and the Bill of Rights put together." He turns to me, a glimmer of hope flickering in his eyes. "But if we can win it fast, it'd be quite strategic and improve our standing in the world."

"Jemmy, we must trust the War Hawks." I place my hand over his. "They're convinced we can take Canada right away without any effort at all."

"I certainly hope they're right. I've only got a year until it's time to gear up for re-election." Oh, the poor man. He's never sounded quite so glum.

"Surely, it'll be over by then, and we'll be busy expanding northward in droves." I smile. "Just think of the many lovely furs I'll buy!"

Instead of his usual chuckle, he stares off with vacant eyes. His agony hurts my heart, so I switch to another tactic.

"Jemmy, remember, plenty of Colonists opposed the War of Independence. They were proven wrong, very wrong. One day history will be kind to you, I'm sure of it."

"I hope my calculated gamble pays off." He takes a deep breath. "I pray that our country will emerge from this war stronger than ever."

For the rest of our bumpy journey down Pennsylvania Avenue, we ride in silence as I squeeze his hand. His worries are far bigger than any one man can handle.

CHAPTER 13
THE TURMOIL OF WAR

Although necessary to ensure our nation's survival, the Second War of Independence proves more dreadful than anyone anticipated. Right from the start, the Federalists dub it "Mr. Madison's War" instead of supporting our national cause against a brutal enemy. The mutual loathing between the factions reaches a whole new level of hostility. As a result, our precious country tears even further apart according to regional differences.

The ardent Republican supporters in the South and out West fire their cannons, organize patriotic parades, and set off grand illuminations. In contrast, the New Englanders go into full-fledged mourning. They fly their flags at half-mast, toll their church bells like there's a funeral, and close their shops for days. In Baltimore, violence breaks out against the editor of a Federalist newspaper. My heart hurts when horrible riots erupt. The mob brutality lasts for days, culminating in the murder of a beloved hero from the Revolution which brings me to tears.

Within a few weeks, Jemmy receives an unexpected letter

by courier. "What in the world? This makes no sense," he gasps, staring down at the communication from the British. "Oh my," he mumbles as he reads it over again while shaking his head. Then he stands up, drops the paper, and watches it flutter to the floor.

"What is it, Jemmy?" I ask, baffled.

"After five years of impressing our sailors, they've finally decided to repeal their policy," he responds, his tone flat.

"Huzzah! That's excellent news, isn't it? That's just what we want!" I stare at him, confused by his lack of jubilance.

"But the letter is dated a few days before we declared war. It's taken weeks to cross the Atlantic." He pinches his lips together. "Now it's totally invalid."

"Oh." My stomach plummets.

"If only I waited a few more weeks." His shoulders sag. "But the War Hawks hounded me for so long."

"There was no way of knowing, Jemmy." I shake my head. "You spent years trying to reason with the Brits, and they rebuffed you every time."

THE WAR PROCEEDS IN A HORRIBLE FASHION. BRITISH SHIPS establish an embargo along the East Coast, paralyzing all trade which further strangles our injured economy. Needless to say, this dire situation distresses us to no end. We are now at their mercy, and those fiends refuse to show us any. I want to hide behind the gowns in my closet and cry, but I must show a brave face for the sake of our nation.

To my great horror, we receive letters every day containing threats to kill us. Spies lurk in our midst, even men who dress themselves as women and try to steal Jemmy's confidential State papers. Unfortunately, the army's enlistment numbers are quite low, and then to make matters worse, desertion becomes a huge problem. Although it goes against his principles, Jemmy decides to pardon all the wayward soldiers. The reality is quite unfortunate. We are so desperate for soldiers that we must even welcome the deserters back into our ranks.

The poor dear is never able to sleep. I smell his tallow candle burning all night long as he reads, plans, and worries until the sun rises. Then almost without fail, more bad news awaits us the next day. Overcome with exhaustion, he falls out of the carriage and knocks his knee out of place at the Capitol. The obnoxious Federalists use this as yet another excuse to mock him in the cruelest fashion as he hobbles about on crutches, wincing with every step. They hurl every insult in the world at him, from calling him a national traitor to declaring him a pygmy.

I bristle at their vicious attacks, and my cheeks grow hot. How dare they challenge Jemmy's loyalty to America? How shortsighted are our fickle countrymen? He's dedicated his entire life to serving our country built on lofty democratic ideals. After all, he's the Father of our Constitution, author of the Bill of Rights, and a four-term Congressman, as well as his countless other contributions over the past thirty-eight years. Their lack of gratitude borders on treason.

"The Federalists have the absolute right to criticize me and my policies without fear of imprisonment or trial," Jemmy insists, remaining firm in his principles. "Otherwise, our Constitution means nothing, and this was all for naught."

"But aren't you offended?" I sputter, incredulous.

"Of course, my dear. I am human after all, despite what they say about me." He cracks a fleeting smile. I'd give anything for it to last just a second longer.

"So, why don't you make them stop then?" I persist in a shrill voice, still not satisfied. "It's damaging the war effort.

Everyone should be coming together right now, not tearing each other apart."

"It's important we fight this war without limiting the rights of our citizens, especially free speech. These adverse conditions are the greatest test for liberty and the Constitution, so dear to us all." Jemmy reflects for a moment, resting his head on his fist. "Like I wrote in the *Federalist Papers*, if men were angels, no government would be necessary." He lowers his voice. "And the Federalists are certainly no angels."

I laugh and give up. He is the president after all—we definitely agree on that.

Unfortunately, the November election looms on the horizon. As if Jemmy doesn't have enough worries, he must also run for office again during these bleak times. Of course, his good manners still prevent him from campaigning, but I'm happy to work behind the scenes and plan social events galore.

My latest tactic is to host more parties with tastier punch, more cookies and cakes, and even better music. Before the war, I often entertained three hundred enthusiastic guests at my squeezes, but now the crowd soars to a whopping five hundred. Honestly, I've never seen such throngs of people and am worn out. Of course, I rally for both Jemmy's sake and our divided country.

In the late spring of 1813, my cousin and Jemmy's Secretary, Edward Coles, becomes deathly ill and heads to Philadelphia for treatment. To my delight, Jemmy asks me to step in and fill the gap. Among my other duties, I am now privy to his Cabinet meetings. When they urge him to delay the presidential election because of the war, he refuses to consider the idea. Then they have the nerve to press him again. Good heavens! Don't they understand the rule of law on which this country was founded not so long ago?

"Absolutely not," he declares in a firm voice. "Taking such

an unconstitutional action, however well-intentioned given our present circumstances, could open the door to blatant corruption during future generations." After all, he is a Founding Father who helped establish the guiding tenets of our republic. I am so thankful he is the one leading us through this turbulent era.

When troops walk by the President's House on their way to the encampment at President's Park, I flag them down and insist they come inside for a visit. Then I serve a mouth-watering array of treats washed down with plentiful cups of Madeira wine. Once the fellows relax, I assure them that their commander in chief has everything under control. If only that was the truth!

Thankfully they don't realize that I'm fibbing. After all, Congress failed to renew Hamilton's National Bank last year. Thus, we have no funding for this hateful war, and the Army suffers from a pathetic dearth of soldiers. Even worse, the Royal Navy's ships outnumber us thirty-to-one which chills me to my core.

By the time the trees shed their leaves, we need some distraction from the grim news trickling in from Canada. Our blunders pile up, each more discouraging than the last. Good heavens, the Army proves itself beyond incompetent. Many soldiers truly are grandfathers who haven't worn a uniform since the War of Independence ended thirty years ago. Much to our dismay, they prove more dangerous to themselves than our enemy. When bombarded, they retreat. Then the situation gets even worse when some refuse to cross the border at all. It's humiliating. Unfortunately, the War Hawks couldn't have been more wrong when they insisted the Canadians would welcome "liberation" from the oppressive British rule.

Eventually we must accept that our three lines of attack on Canada are all an abysmal failure. However, the worst loss takes place at Fort Detroit in August. Without firing a single shot, Revolutionary veteran General Hull surrenders his army of 2,500 soldiers to a British force with less than 700 troops. Outraged, the *National Intelligencer* denounces him as a booby. Even his own soldiers curse him, calling him both a traitor and a coward to his face.

Within minutes of getting word, we abandon our summer stay at Montpelier and race back to Washington City. Poor Sukey and Paul are crushed to leave their families without saying goodbye, especially Paul who's smitten with a slave girl named Fanny over at Greenfield. However, it must be done. Soon an Army court-martial convicts General Hull of cowardice and neglect of duty. When he is sentenced to be shot, Jemmy rejects that punishment. We also suffer dismal losses at Niagara in western New York, Montreal, and the Northwest Territory. Morale sags so low there is none left, only despair.

As we arrive back breathless in Washington City, our Navy surprises the entire world with an astounding victory. Through an amazing coincidence, General Hull's own nephew, Navy Captain Hull, resurrects our sagging spirits with his uncanny success. Under his courageous command, he takes the USS *Constitution* into battle against the HMS *Guerriere* off the coast of Nova Scotia. The British bombard the old frigate named by General Washington with a flurry of eighteen-pound British cannonballs. However, the missiles just bounce off the *Constitution*'s wooden hull. An amazed sailor shouts, "It's as if the ship was made of iron instead of oak."

Within thirty minutes, the *Guerriere* surrenders to the *Constitution*. Huzzah! From that moment on, the *Constitution* is heralded as Old Ironsides. Even the sullen Federalists in New England cheer at this unexpected success. Against all odds, our tiny Navy emerges victorious over the world's greatest sea power—at least in one battle. It's truly a miracle.

"The Navy's USS *Constitution* is as iron-clad as our country's Constitution!" Jemmy declares, brimming with unusually good cheer.

CHAPTER 14
THE NAVY BALL AND JEMMY'S SECOND INAUGURATION
OCTOBER 1812 - APRIL 1813

Spurred on by our recent triumph, Congress finally votes to expand the Navy and orders the Navy Yard to construct two new warships, the USS *Columbia* and the USS *Argus*.

The Secretary of the Navy celebrates with a lavish ball in December, right before the election. Ah, the mere thought of a happy occasion brings the first genuine smile to my face in months. What an oasis of joy amidst a desert of sorrows. Of course, it is the opposite for Jemmy.

"I'm far too tense to attend with voting about to start," he demurs.

"Quite understandable, darling." I pat his arm. "I will be honored to represent us both."

"I suppose it is no secret by now that you thrive on public events while I do not." He shakes his head.

"We all have our gifts, Jemmy." I wring my hands, wishing there was something I could do or say to console him.

As Sukey helps me dress for the event, Jemmy forces the corners of his lips upward. "My dearest, you look ravishing." He ponders for a moment. "And I do believe a lovely scent of lilac lingers in the air." He never ceases to amaze me. Even in his gloomiest moments as this gut-wrenching war limps along, he is still such a fine man.

A most wonderful surprise awaits everyone at the ball. As I mingle with the partygoers, a flurry of footsteps pound outside the entrance, mixed with excited voices. When the band strikes up an animated version of 'Yankee Doodle,' four senior Navy Officers dash into the ballroom. They look quite dapper in their dress uniforms of dark blue coats with neat rows of buttons and stylish white pantaloons. With great ceremony, they unfurl a massive British flag to wild applause. Then they march it all around the room on their shoulders, flying it like a canopy between them.

When they finally reach me, they get down on a bended knee and lay it at my feet with a flourish. Then they proclaim in unison, "We present this flag to you, Queen Dolley, from the mast of Great Britain's largest frigate, the HMS *Macedonian*."

Overcome with joy, I burst into tears.

The crowd breaks out in a roar loud enough to ruin my hearing. Of course, I cry out too and give the Navy Officers a round of hugs and kisses. After all, these victorious sailors traveled four days nonstop just to deliver it to me at the ball. Ah, the Navy has delivered yet another miracle all the way from the Canary Islands, boosting everyone's spirits, including mine. Even more importantly, this unexpected victory clinches Jemmy's precarious bid for re-election. I am so thankful for both events.

I insist on bringing the flag home to distract Jemmy from his troubles. When I parade it around his study and lay it at his feet with a wobbly curtsy, he flashes a wan smile. However, his eyes sparkle with a tinge of merriment which heartens me. Alas, he forbids me from bringing it to bed, so I hang it over our footboard so we can admire it as we doze off, hoping to foster pleasant dreams for just one night.

To our great relief, Jemmy prevails in his re-election bid. However, he wins by less votes than during the previous election. I do believe my efforts made a difference. During the campaign, a Senator from Kentucky even called me the real candidate, declaring in a cheeky fashion, "Mrs. Madison made a very good president and must not be turned out." Of course, one of Jemmy's many Federalist critics gripes, "Mrs. Madison saved the administration of her husband."

Although our country is still mired in this calamitous war, I take great pains to ensure the pageantry of Jemmy's second inauguration in March 1813 matches his first, scheduling a lovely reception at the President's House afterwards. Especially during these dark times, the establishment of American traditions is crucial. They link us back to our inspiring beginnings and loop us into our uncertain future. It's like passing the Olympic torch with its mystical flame.

During the ceremony, his new Vice President, Elbridge Gerry, sits to his left with Chief Justice Marshall on his right, wearing his black robe once again. In his trademark black suit, Jemmy gives his inaugural address, still rocking on his heels. He attempts to show national confidence as he calls upon the smiles of Heaven to end the war. Everyone still struggles to hear him, and then the Chief Justice administers the second oath of office, towering over Jemmy just as before.

At my insistence, we hold a festive inaugural ball at Davis's Hotel at 601 Pennsylvania Avenue, an extended row of Federal-style townhouses. After an elaborate meal, I introduce a delicious new flavor of iced creams for dessert—strawberry. Of course, I pretend to be merry. Sometimes I am so busy acting that I have no idea what I really feel. Perhaps that is for the best.

Just a month later in April, our troops pull off a surprising military success. They prevail over the Brits in York, the Capital of Upper Canada, despite our enemies' vast experience. After all, they have been fighting Napoleon for more than a decade. My chest swells with pride, but the euphoria is short-lived. Giddy with the unfamiliar taste of victory, our troops disobey orders, loot the city, and burn York's public buildings. Unfortunately, this rampage raises tensions with our neighbors to the north even higher.

Jemmy condemns their atrocious conduct right away, but the damage remains. A seething Canada demands vengeance on the United States. Oh, how I want to run and hide my head in the farthest fields of Montpelier. But I, too, must soldier on and support our determined President Madison.

Needless to say, Jemmy and I are frustrated with these unsettling developments, but we maintain an upbeat attitude for the public's sake. If the American people discovered the true depth of our despair, a nationwide panic would erupt.

"Jefferson was only partly right that the presidency is splendid misery," Jemmy complains behind closed doors in a moment of weakness. "It's just misery. There's nothing splendid about it."

With tears in my eyes, I have to agree.

However, just when I'm convinced the situation can't get any worse, it does. As I deliver coffee and cake to Jemmy's study, Treasury Secretary Gallatin announces, "We hardly have enough money to last until the end of the month." His voice trembles. "The Treasury is bare."

I nearly drop the tray, but recover and carry on as I must, staying to partake in the refreshments.

"I'll admit it," Jemmy replies in a low voice. "Hamilton's Federalist vision was right after all—at least in one regard. God rest his soul. Why in the world did Jefferson and I ever oppose the National Bank? Having one now would certainly help the common people."

"We must all learn from our mistakes and move forward." I respond, determined to bolster him with positivity. "Remember how you first believed the Bill of Rights was unnecessary? But you took some time to reflect on it and changed your mind. Then to your credit, you became its very architect."

CHAPTER 15
THE ENEMY OCCUPIES OUR SHORES
SPRING & SUMMER 1813

Come spring of 1813, the dreaded Rear Admiral George Cockburn arrives in our midst, eager to retaliate for our soldiers' appalling misconduct in York. His massive fleet blockades the great Chesapeake Bay that stretches two-hundred miles from Maryland to Virginia. From his base at Fort Albion on Tangier Island, the arrogant warmonger terrorizes our citizens with barbaric raids along the coast, either destroying or stealing everything in his path.

The lout even robs petrified women and children of the clothing right off their backs. "Why must you scare us and our families?" asks a sobbing girl at one point.

"You must ask your President Jemmy Madison," the evil Cockburn replies with an imperious scowl. "He invited us here."

When Cockburn spies an American flag flying over Havre de Grace, Maryland, he torches the entire town, including forty of its sixty houses. He earns America's hatred overnight and becomes known as the Beast of Havre de Grace and House-burn the Monster.

A furious Jemmy is determined to end the torment of

these defenseless small towns along the Chesapeake. He dispatches our Russian ambassador John Quincy Adams and Treasury Secretary Gallatin to St. Petersburg, Russia, for negotiations with the British. He sends Payne along to assist the delegation. Although our boy shows no enthusiasm for such a wonderful opportunity, we hope this will make a man out of him and perhaps a future diplomat as well. After all, John Quincy Adams accompanied his father overseas as a boy, helping him evolve into a gifted statesman.

The British scoundrels sink the USS *Chesapeake* in June. Spectators line the rooftops in Boston, watching the enormous carnage as it unfolds close to their shore. With his last words, the captain exclaims, "Don't give up the ship." Despite our heartbreaking loss, this becomes America's rallying cry.

Of course, I seethe over Cockburn's savage methods of warfare, but I refuse to let him intimidate me. At my next squeeze, I address our anxious crowd, brimming with confidence. "Cockburn calculates these silly excursions precisely to send our country into a state of alarm. They can threaten us all they want, but we shall still be festive. Please enjoy today's special Chesapeake Whiskey Punch."

❧

AFTER A YEAR FILLED WITH NONSTOP DISASTERS, MY POOR Jemmy is worn out, understandably so. By June, he contracts a horrible case of malaria. The severe fever renders him unable to sleep and also saps him of his energy and appetite. His sickness rages more than three weeks as he lingers between life and death. He suffers from both chills and vomiting and then sweats for days. Once he survives that torture, the same gruesome cycle repeats itself over and over again.

I stir Peruvian ground bark into a glass of wine. Then I

force him to swallow the bitter concoction, feeding it to him spoonful by spoonful. Of course, I cancel my squeezes and nurse him like a baby. I may lose my precious Jemmy to the pressures of this Herculean job, but I don't have the time for despair. To make matters even worse, our new Vice President Gerry falls ill as well. Rumors swirl as people speculate who will become our next president.

Horrible memories flood my mind from the yellow fever epidemic twenty years ago. I cared for my husband John and our sick baby around the clock then, too. Despite my best efforts, I lost them both to that dreadful disease and then contracted it myself, along with Payne. I pray the Grim Reaper won't destroy my family yet again. When I finally manage to sleep for a few hours, my brain is far too exhausted to conjure up any nightmares. For that I am thankful, but I live with fear all day long.

When I retreat to change my frock after Jemmy's latest bout of vomit lands on me, Congressman Daniel Webster takes that opportunity to elbow his way into the sick room. As Jemmy suffers an awful case of the chills, this nasty man has the nerve to berate him about the war. After he leaves, he ridicules Jemmy in public for wearing a nightcap during the summer heat.

"I understand the importance of the Bill of Rights, I really do," I vent to Jemmy. "But at times like these, though, I can't help but favor limits to free speech." I have never been so angry in my life.

Jemmy shakes his head with more spirit than he's shown in weeks. Of course, he doesn't agree with me. I knew he wouldn't.

"Even though you're the butt of every joke in Washington City?" I throw up my hands.

"Yes, it's a good thing the Constitution doesn't cover common decency," he wisecracks with a wan smile. "All the

Federalists would be in jail." Then he breaks into a spasm of coughing as I pat his back and enjoy a much-needed laugh myself. "After all, the Preamble starts with 'We the People of the United States.' That includes everyone, whether we like it or not."

With my next breath, I instruct Sukey to pack for Montpelier. Her face lights up, overjoyed to reunite with her family after such a lengthy absence. Jemmy needs some native air to restore his health. Just as important, though, I must leave town before I throttle Mr. Webster. I am ecstatic to leave the viperous tongues and oppressive humidity behind in our wagon tracks. I need a moment of peace, but that proves elusive.

⚜

AFTER A FIVE-DAY SOJOURN OVER ROUGH ROADS TO Montpelier and then two more weeks of utter hell dealing with Jemmy's illness, his dismal condition finally improves. For a few hours every day, I seat him on the front porch. He enjoys the hazy blue mountains that stretch all the way into eternity and the occasional lightning storms in the late afternoons. He regains a bit of color which lifts my beleaguered soul.

Now that he is finally on the mend, I fear for my own death from overwhelming fatigue, but I can't let on. Jemmy's well-being has always been shaky, but it's far worse now during his precarious recovery. He doesn't need to worry about me as well.

An inspiring tale of defiance sweeps the country in August, bolstering us. Under the cover of darkness, the British bullies sail into the harbor of St. Michaels, Maryland. They are determined to unleash their cannons on this town known for its shipbuilding. However, the residents devise an ingenious plan to save it. They snuff out every candle and then hang their bright lanterns in the treetops on the outskirts. As a result, the British gunners overshoot the village and are unable to inflict any damage.

"Ah, their gumption gives me the strength to carry on," I write to Hannah Gallatin. "Our eventual success will show Mr. Madison to the world as he really is, one of the best leaders, as well as the greatest men on Earth."

Then in September, America rejoices when the USS *Niagara* defeats five enemy ships on Lake Erie, using a risky technique. The triumphant Captain Perry declares, "We have met the enemy, and they are ours." This decisive victory allows us to recover Fort Detroit a few days later. Perhaps even more important, it spurs Jemmy to regain his lost vigor. Soon he is back to his old self, much to my relief. We head back to Washington City and reunite with his rejuvenated secretary, Edward Coles.

The loathsome Cockburn's assaults on the Chesapeake continue throughout the fall, but he never makes any attempt to approach Washington City. I feel vindicated. Just as I believed, his vile threats are empty. He wouldn't dream of entering our capital city. What a thrashing we would give that villain!

Like an actress, I maintain my daily routine of gaiety. Nevertheless, a paralyzing weight of anxiety hangs over us all throughout the long winter. We remain wary, dreading the stormy new year that awaits us. Come 1814, Cockburn's return is inevitable.

CHAPTER 16
HORRIBLE NEWS
WINTER - JULY, 1814

Over the winter, Jemmy dispatches our delegation to make the arduous journey to Russia so that Czar Alexander can mediate a peace settlement with the British. However, by the time they reach the other side of the world, the Brits have departed. This cruel trick not only dashes our high hopes, but it also embarrasses us on the world stage, achieving their underhanded goal.

Then in April 1814, they taunt us again. Now they insist on meeting in Ghent, Belgium. Determined not to become the international laughingstock a second time, Jemmy summons Speaker Clay to his study and asks him to meet our delegation there and end the war once and for all.

Realizing this requires him to resign as Speaker of the House, Clay agrees with some reluctance. "Well, I helped start this war, so I'm duty-bound to help end it," he admits to me, stopping to chat on his way out of Jemmy's study. Looking a bit dazed, he runs a hand through his hair.

Later that afternoon, Betsy Bonaparte and I enjoy a chat in my cozy parlor. Sukey serves us coffee and ginger pound cake as we discuss Jane Austen's popular new novel, *Pride and*

Prejudice. While I enjoy a thick slice, Betsy nibbles away at a tiny one, preserving her delicate figure. Of course, I have no idea that we will soon receive the worst news of all.

"Betsy, thank you so much for coming to visit. This distraction from my worries is such a welcome treat."

"My pleasure, truly." She smiles. "I'm always happy to get away from Baltimore which I find so dull. It's not the same without Payne there," she confesses, taking a dainty sip of coffee. "I miss stopping by St. Mary's to check on him and his studies. I've come to think of him as my second son."

"You are so dear, Betsy. Yes, I wish he was still there, too. You kept such a close eye and taught him so much about etiquette, not to mention saving his French grade. I doubt he would've passed without your tutoring."

"He and I share a love for the finer things in life, so he made great company for me." She sighs with a wistful expression.

"Well, we haven't heard from him since he left for Russia, so I'm fretting about that," I confide. "Without any mediations actually taking place, work hasn't been occupying his time. I pray he is faring well." Frowning, I look down at my crumb-covered napkin.

"I'm sure you'll hear from him any day now," she reassures me, looking out toward the Potomac. "With both wars going on these days, it's so hard getting letters from Europe. It takes forever to get word back and forth."

"Yes, you're right, honey." I tap her on the knee. "That makes me feel so much better." I take a gander at her gauzy new dress and gush, "What a lovely gown. At least Baltimore has some lovely boutiques. How I wish Washington City had at least one decent shop."

"*Tisk, tisk.* You poor dear." She pats my hand as she shakes her head. "Would you like me to pick up something pretty for you? My favorite place is called French Gloves Fashion; they have such stylish things there. Of course, it's a far cry from anything in Europe," she scoffs.

"Oh Betsy, you are such a gem to offer. I just adore the lovely cape you sent me. It kept me so warm throughout the winter." I turn to face her. "Actually, I am looking for some white gloves. It's so difficult to keep them clean, even with Sukey at her best. I'd also love a gown with lace flowers in either gold or silver." Then I add, "And anything elegant in the form of a turban."

"But of course," she replies, giving me a gentle nudge. After all, unique headpieces are my trademark.

When the front bell rings nonstop, Sukey hurries to the door and opens it with her usual impeccable manners. However, our impatient caller plows right into it, slamming it back against the wall. A disheveled messenger bursts inside and rushes by us without even a glance. Then he sprints up the stairs to Jemmy's office, three steps at a time.

"What in the world was that?" I exclaim, staring over my shoulder.

Within seconds, the courier stumbles back down the flight, gulping in air, and sees himself out.

Betsy and I stare at each other and hold our breath.

Soon Jemmy's light footsteps plod down the stairs, stopping for a moment to rest after each step. Then he all but staggers into the parlor with his eyes bugging out. "I just received an overseas dispatch. It's good news for the world but wretched for America," he blurts, not even acknowledging our beloved friend. Droplets of sweat run down his sweet face, now even paler than at his first inauguration.

"My God, what now?" Horrified, I jump to my feet and clap a hand to my chest.

"The Duke of Wellington has finally toppled Napoleon. The Brits have sent him into exile on Elba Island in Italy." He gives a weary sigh. "So, the Crown will turn their full might on us, their only enemy. From now on, we will fight the world's mightiest military alone."

"Oh, no," I gasp as my stomach plummets. "What horrible news!"

"I have no doubt Cockburn will arrive back in the Chesapeake any day to ransack more villages." He winces. "Now he'll be even more determined to avenge our attack on York." He shakes his head. "But the irony rankles me to my core. Now that their war with France is over, they no longer have any need to kidnap our sailors."

"Well, at least my former brother-in-law is gone." Betsy finally stands up and tosses her head. "Now I can finally travel to Europe and enjoy some culture. And this time I can actually get off the ship."

What selfishness while the fate of our beloved country hangs in the balance! I stifle the urge to scold her. Instead, I smile and grab both of their hands. We stand there in silence, digesting the weighty news. Such is the melancholy of war—together yet so alone.

As Jemmy predicted, Cockburn resumes his campaign in the Chesapeake with renewed cruelty. His latest act of savagery makes the headline of the *National Intelligencer*: Three young sisters beg him not to burn their house, so he grants them ten minutes to remove their belongings. The sixteen-year-old drops to his feet and begs for mercy, but he just stares at his watch. When the time elapses, his officer weeps with the girls as the flames consume their home.

Full of outrage, Jemmy offers a thousand-dollar reward for capturing this savage, dead or alive, as well as five hundred for each ear. He also warns of a potential attack on Washington City. However, the pompous Secretary of War Armstrong disagrees, declaring, "By God, they will certainly not come here. What the devil will they do here? No! No! Baltimore is the place, our third largest city. It's on the coast without any forests or God-forsaken swamps to contend with. I can assure you; this is all unnecessary alarm."

Thankfully I feel no agitation. After all, the crisis isn't anywhere near us. We resist the useless anxiety and carry on with our everyday lives. To make my confidence known, I entertain all the more. Even Margaret assures me, "There is so little apprehension of danger for Washington City."

I jot down the latest update to my precious son in Belgium, chagrined that I still haven't received any correspondence from him.

My Dear Payne,

The British are now on our shores, plundering private property, but rarely coming to battle. And when they do, they're always beaten. I'm confident that if the war lasts six more months, the United States will conquer her enemies.

-Mother

By July, the enemy starts to advance toward Washington City. Jemmy orders the city to make full preparations to defend itself, but Secretary of War Armstrong ignores him. For the first time, a twinge of apprehension passes through me. Rather than burden Jemmy, though, I confide in Hannah instead. "How I wish we were safe in Philadelphia." As usual, it is my duty to maintain a strong face for everyone else.

Cockburn blusters about "making his bow" in my drawing rooms as the new ruler of Washington City. Then the ruthless swine threatens to put me in chains and force me on a humiliating parade through the streets of London. Needless to say, fear and alarm abound here in Washington City. As for me, I am not rattled, but I do resent him making personal threats against me.

Margaret fills the *National Intelligencer* with sensational stories of the British atrocities, including their vicious attacks on women. Since Armstrong still brushes off their threats, Jemmy creates the new Military District of Washington City and appoints General Winder to head it.

On the Fourth of July, I celebrate America's thirty-eighth birthday with my biggest squeeze yet. Unfortunately, the summer is already unbearably hot with hundred-degree temperatures, so the servants open the windows and distribute fans to our perspiring guests as they arrive. I debut a fresh look, my hair in ringlets and a turban decorated with sprigs of green wheat. As usual, I praise our heroes and insist on the full presentation of our military colors.

Then I address the crowd, downplaying the second British expedition wreaking havoc so close to us. "Sweet friends, this is just overheated rhetoric once again."

Spurred on by my confidence, our guests respond with great applause and indulge themselves in hours of merriment. They cast their worries aside, but I guard mine close to my heart.

CHAPTER 17
THE ENEMY ADVANCES
AUGUST 1814

To my great horror, the largest British fleet yet sails into Chesapeake Bay in mid-August with 4,500 seasoned veterans, fresh from conquering the French. Their fifty ships head up the Patuxent River without any opposition and land in Benedict, Maryland. Goodness gracious, the enemy is now only forty-five miles from Washington City. Our home at Montpelier is twice as far away! A tingling sensation ripples down my spine, but I arch my back and shake it off.

"Unless you leave now, Mrs. Madison, the house will be burned over your head," taunts the loathsome Cockburn. I refuse to allow this new threat to fuel any anxiety.

To Jemmy's growing frustration, the ever-stubborn Secretary Armstrong still refuses to deploy the militia. He insists that Baltimore is their only target and ridicules the possibility of an attack on Washington City.

"I will be the first to admit that our preparations for defense may be dismally inadequate. Even so, it's impossible for Cockburn to get his army here," I declare, maintaining my defiant attitude.

Alas, he does.

As the massive influx of British troops marches toward us, Armstrong still refuses to acknowledge Washington City's vulnerability. Beyond disgusted, Jemmy would love to fire him, but he doesn't have time to find a replacement. Furious locals threaten Jemmy that if he tries to flee the city, they'll stop him in his tracks and make him fall with it.

Despite these awful threats, I am nothing but confident. In fact, I am far more outraged than alarmed. However, I do keep my old Tunisian sword under my bed within an arm's reach. As a former Quaker, I was raised a pacifist. However, I do believe in fighting back when attacked.

On August 23, I carry on as if nothing is amiss, hosting my usual dinner party for thirty guests at three o'clock. The tasty meal includes turkey, fish, pickled eggs, puff pops, green beans, and Virginia potatoes with ham and onions.

Unfortunately, this broiling summer has been the hottest anyone can remember. Due to the oppressive heat, I serve apricot iced creams for dessert. This cools us down for a delightful minute or two.

Little do I suspect this is the last full day we will ever spend here in the President's House. However, as the grandfather clock strikes midnight, a messenger pounds on the door, believing we are in a deep sleep. If only that was true. As we hover around the door in our dressing gowns, he thrusts a note into Jemmy's shaking hands.

President Madison:

The British are in full march for Washington. Have the materials prepared to destroy the northern bridges and the Navy Yard. And you better remove the records. Our militiamen shall sleep on the floor of the Hall of Representatives tonight.

—Sec of State Monroe

. . .

"DEAR GOD, THIS IS IT," BREATHES JEMMY, HIS FACE ASHEN. "I never should've trusted Armstrong."

Needless to say, the rest of our night is sleepless. Our gnashing of the teeth is interspersed with constant tossing and turning. At dawn, the sun has the nerve to rise like it's an ordinary day, already sending off more scorching rays of heat. Kicking off the damp sheets that are twisted into knots, we force our weary bodies out of bed, and kneel. At this point my sore knee is the least of my concerns. We beseech God to show mercy on our young country. Today we must face our worst fears. The same British army that defeated Emperor Napoleon now advances upon tiny Washington City.

"Dearest, I'm sending word to Mr. Pleasanton over at the State Department to take action." Jemmy looks over at me, his bloodshot eyes threatening to spill over in a waterfall.

"Why? What does that mean?" I grab his arm, dreading his response.

He holds his breath for a moment and then releases it. "We must move the Founding Documents to a safe location."

"Dear God, has it really come to this?" I can hardly breathe.

"Not to worry, my dear. It's just a precaution, but we can't risk losing the Declaration of Independence, the Constitution or the Bill of Rights." He purses his lips together. "Now I must go with Armstrong and Winder to join the troops in Bladensburg."

"But darling, are you sure it's safe for you there? Shouldn't you stay back?"

"It may not be the most prudent move, but it's the right thing to do. I can't ask our militiamen to risk their lives on the battlefield if their president is too afraid to show his face there." He shrugs. "Gallatin lent me some dueling pistols."

Convinced my bookish husband has lost his mind, I lose my patience. "Make sure to stay back! You are not a solider. You've never even fired a musket because of your epilepsy. You are our president. The most important thing is for you to stay alive and out of enemy hands. Just think of the morale if something awful happens to you." I swallow a lump in my throat. "Like becoming their prisoner—or worse."

"Yes, dear. You're right, as always." He holds my hand and asks in a husky voice, "Do you have the courage?"

Putting a hand to his chest, he stops himself. "I apologize, my darling. You are the bravest person I know, including myself." He pauses again. "But I wonder if you have the firmness to remain here until I return. I can arrange an escort to Virginia now if you would like."

I don't hesitate for a second. "I have no fear but for you and the success of our Army." That is God's honest truth. "However, I do have utmost confidence in you both. In fact, I've already invited forty guests for a victory dinner this afternoon at three. Everyone has responded yes. We will await you, the Generals, and your Cabinet when you return here in triumph."

"All right, my dearest." His shoulders slump, like he is literally bending under the weight of his worries. They are far too heavy, no matter his genius and tireless dedication. "I hate to ride off and leave you here, but one hundred soldiers now stand outside to protect you and the President's House above all else." He looks up at me with tears in his haggard eyes once again. "I beseech you. Please take care of yourself and my Cabinet papers above all else. But you are most important."

"Of course, my love." This wonderful man never ceases to amaze me.

"And if anything goes awry—" He cuts himself off and then continues, "I've arranged for Mr. Carroll to come from

Georgetown and escort you back over to Belle Vue himself. God willing, we'll meet up there and take the Little Falls Bridge over to Wiley's Tavern."

I nod, although I believe with all my heart it won't come to that. It just can't.

He finally departs, a cloud of dust rising behind his carriage, as I cry out, "I hold out hope!"

I stand firm in my resolve, and my heart is free of fear. I am determined to remain in the Great Castle until his return.

Whirling around, I spring into action and preoccupy myself with the usual dinner preparations. "Paul, please set the dinner table for forty guests at our usual three o'clock with our best crystal glasses. We'll have Mr. Madison's favorite meal. Let's prepare three huge Virginia hams with green peas, corn oysters, Madison rolls and fairy butter, followed by peach cobbler. Do bring up the fine wine, ale, and cider from the cellar. Cool the wine in the decanters on the sideboard. And then put a candle in every window. I'll have you and Sukey light them to celebrate their victory right before Mr. Madison arrives."

CHAPTER 18

WASHINGTON CITY UNDER SIEGE

MORNING OF AUGUST 24, 1814

Red-faced messengers arrive in a flurry, delivering a slew of cancellations from our dinner guests. Each note feels like a bitter blow to my anxious heart. Finally, I must accept the reality of the situation. My friends and acquaintances have fled, every last one of them. However, I have no idea where they went. Presumably they headed south over the Potomac, putting a river between them and the nasty British marching down from Maryland. No one made even tentative plans to evacuate, not even me, thanks to Secretary Armstrong's outrageous insistence that the Brits had no interest in Washington City. How I would love to box his ears right now!

At this point, our nation's capital lies wide open with no defenses in place. Even the hundred guards that Jemmy ordered to defend the President's House have vanished, melting into the fray. They waited until I turned my back and then joined the frantic exodus like the Red Sea parting for a second time. It's unnerving to say the least, but I don't blame them. How I'd love to sneak away from this living nightmare.

Somehow, though, I must carry on. I remain determined to wait for Jemmy.

I can't allow a glimmer of the fear wracking my soul to seep out. Regardless of their current whereabouts, my countrymen will demand to know my every move during this crisis. They need to trust my unwavering dedication to them. Hopefully that will inspire them to keep their faith in Jemmy and me. Of course, history will be the ultimate judge of my actions. No matter how great the temptation to flee alongside these panicked masses, I won't allow any American to call me a deserter or, worse yet, a traitor.

I race to the roof in my dressing gown and slippers, careful not to wake Anna and the children. Richard already left before dawn to join the militia. I turn my spyglass and look from every possible angle at least a hundred times. I hope with every fiber of my being to spot my darling husband riding home on his white horse. I envision him dressed for glory in his commander in chief hat, flanked by his Cabinet whom I pray have finally risen to the occasion. How I look forward to hearing his rollicking tales of defeating the foolhardy British, perhaps just minutes away.

However, hours pass. There I am, still up on the roof, holding my spyglass in one hand and slapping at blood-thirsty mosquitos with the other. My eagle's view of the utter pandemonium below mesmerizes me. Despite witnessing the rampant suffering taking place, I can't tear my eyes away. I wish with my whole heart that Jemmy's slight frame will dash into view any second, ending this interminable waiting.

The punishing sun beats down, merciless in its intensity. It's like an oven that won't stop. Sweat soaks through my gray Quaker-style work dress. My arms turn bright pink from the piercing rays with raised bumps from the mosquitos feasting on me. Jemmy jokes that my sweetness attracts them, but perhaps it is the many sweets that I eat. Not a drop of rain has fallen in three weeks, so the mud has transformed into a fine powder that coats people's faces like a mask. Unfortunately, dirt and bug bites are the least of my worries right now.

A manic hodgepodge of carriages, horses, and carts piled high with trunks, feather beds, and prized possessions clog the roads. With their husbands off fighting in the militia, frantic women run pell-mell on foot, weaving in and out of traffic carrying heaping piles of baggage. Others drag overloaded handcarts or push wheelbarrows piled so high they can't see the road in front of them, causing many accidents. Perhaps the most pathetic are those who only had time to slam their front door and now walk along in a daze, empty-handed. Sobbing children trail along behind with no one comforting them. It's a wonder the frightened horses and tall wagon wheels don't crush them.

James Blake, the Mayor of Washington City, gallops up to the house, flailing his arms over his head. Then still on his saddle, he makes a tiny bow and calls up, "Mrs. Madison, I think it would be best for you to go now. I want to keep you safe."

"Thank you, Mayor Blake," I shout back with a contrived cheery smile. "You're so kind to visit, but you needn't worry about me. I'm just fine up here waiting for Mr. Madison to return."

"Yes, ma'am." He frowns. "I understand." Then he gives a quick salute in my direction and charges off.

Starting at one in the afternoon, cannons boom and rockets whizz through the air, setting off a strange red glare. Soon hapless groups of sweaty militiamen in disheveled gray uniforms emerge from the woods and wander in circles on Pennsylvania Avenue. Some run as if being chased while others hobble. The rest creep along like they are still in the midst of a battle. It's such a bizarre sight that at first, I'm bewildered. Then alarm fills my soul.

Why aren't these soldiers still in Bladensburg facing off against the British? No one seems to be in charge, and they don't appear to have a destination. They swarm in and out from all directions, covered head to toe in black dust. However, the most distressing part is their sluggish demeanor. They don't carry muskets or show any intention to defend Washington City from our evil invaders. My spirits sag at this pathetic sight. Perhaps we are doomed to become British subjects once again.

To my great thrill, a message from Jemmy arrives in his flowing ink script. I fly down the stairs to read it several times over.

My Dearest,

Our troops are in high spirits. Reports about the enemy vary by the hour. The latest is that they are not strong and without any cavalry or infantry. I believe we shall easily defeat them. I look forward to your celebratory dinner and being with you this evening.

J

Wiping the sweat from my brow, I nearly swoon with relief. It all makes sense now. The Generals must've released those soldiers who wander the streets. They didn't need them after all.

Mayor Blake appears on the doorstep again, his face drawn. "Why, Mrs. Madison, you're still here."

"Oh yes, I am," I reply, nonchalant. "Yes, indeed." Then I change the subject. "Where's your family? Shouldn't you be attending to them?"

"I sent them off without me." He shakes his head. "I can't

leave, not yet. We're still rounding up men for a last stand to defend the city. I'm posting handbills and handing out flyers, and I put an ad in the newspaper. We're meeting on the steps of the Capitol soon." He pauses. "Please, Mrs. Madison, for your own well-being, I think it's wise for you to depart now."

"I'm fine, really. I just received a message from my husband. Everything is going well. They expect an easy victory."

"I'm afraid I just got word that things have turned for the worse." The mayor's shoulders sag. "I believe it's best to leave as soon as possible." He catches himself. "But of course, it's your choice, Mrs. Madison."

"Thank you so much, Mayor Blake. I truly appreciate your concern, but I'll wait here for my husband as we planned."

"For two years I tried to build fortifications around the city, but that durn Armstrong voted them down every time." He grits his teeth. "At this point, I despise that idiot even more than Cockburn."

I nod, biting hard on my lower lip to prevent myself from criticizing Jemmy's incompetent Secretary of War aloud. A sweet metallic taste fills my mouth, which I realize is blood. Then it turns bitter, matching my feelings.

As Mayor Blake purses his lips and turns to leave a second time, I receive another dispatch from Jemmy. This one is written with pencil in a shaky script.

Dearest,

Be ready to flee at a moment's notice. You must get in your carriage and leave the city now. The enemy is much stronger than reported. They may reach the city with intention to destroy.

J

. . .

My stomach churns as a wave of despair washes over me. What will become of Washington City? Something awful has happened, I'm sure of it. But what? What went wrong? Jemmy's first dispatch was so optimistic. If only the battle was within range of my spyglass, I could find out for myself.

My ears ring as the cannons still roar from Bladensburg. After all, the battle is only four miles away. How times have changed since the celebratory fire that awoke me on the morning of Jemmy's first inauguration only five years ago.

In a moment of desperation, I scratch off a harried letter to Lucy. It is a jumble of words that make no sense, but thinking of her is my only comfort right now.

I cock my head and blink into the blinding sun, recalling that Rosalie Calvert lives in Bladensburg. No doubt her precious Riversdale is near the hostilities in such a tiny town. As much as her mean-spirited comments irk me, I hope she and her young family remain unscathed. I must inquire about their well-being when Jemmy returns.

Worry has never consumed my soul such as it does now. I agonize not only for Jemmy and my loved ones, but for my fellow Americans forced to evacuate without any warning like a pack of dogs with their tails between their legs. As Washington City empties out, our citizens have changed status. They are now refugees.

I turn my spyglass onto the encampment in President's Park, teeming with soldiers who mill around with dazed looks on their dirty faces. Determined to get an update, I tear down the stairs to the front hall. Dressed in miniature military uniforms, my nephews play on their rocking horses near the front door, shooting at each other with brooms.

"No, I'm Uncle Jemmy!" hollers James Madison Cutts.

"But it's my turn," shouts back his younger brother. "You got to be him last time!"

"I've got his name, plus I'm older than you. So, you're General Cockburn again."

Too traumatized to smile, I scurry past them. However, I pat two-year-old Dolley Madison Cutts' curly head as she plays with her ornate dollhouse, a replica of the President's House. How excited I was to give it to her for her recent birthday. She moves the paper doll in my likeness around the house at a frantic pace. Ah, children are such a mirror of their surroundings.

As I speed down the hallway, I glance into Anna's room where she stuffs a mound of clothes into a small valise. I turn my head away; I can't bear the sight. This should not be happening. We should not be scurrying out of Washington City like frightened mice. I despise Armstrong with all my heart. I grit my teeth as the windows rattle and walls shake with each successive blast from the battle.

I race downstairs to the kitchen where the aroma of Madison rolls and peach cobbler wafts through the air. French John, Sukey, and Paul scurry around in a frenzy, scrambling to prepare our victory dinner. With all the commotion, I forgot all about it.

"What on earth?" squawks Polly in an irritated tone, perched on top of a cabinet. Spotting me, she takes flight and lands on my shoulder. Nuzzling my ear, she coos, "Queen Dolley! Queen Dolley!"

For the first time ever, I shake her off and ignore her as she screeches her favorite French swear words at me. I would never dare to repeat them, even in a foreign language.

With a steaming platter of Virginia ham in his hands, French John clears his throat. "Mrs. Madison, I must inform you of something."

"What is it?" I snap.

"Well..." He grimaces.

"Just tell me, John."

"It seems all the guests have cancelled for dinner." He glances down at the humungous ham. "I cannot imagine who is going to eat all this food."

"That is hardly my concern." I throw up my hands. "Get me some news from the battle. I'm terribly worried. Something's definitely amiss."

He hands the massive platter off to Paul who stoops under the weight, and we hustle out to the front steps. I am awestruck as he navigates his way across the congested street like a monkey swinging through banana trees. He pats the nearest filthy soldier on the shoulder and points over at me. The two dodge their way between the caravans back over to me. It's a miracle they make it across in one piece.

Ignoring the rising panic around us, the dazed soldier takes off his sweat-soaked hat and bows to me. His eyes are cast down onto his worn-out boots tied together with frayed rope. Without a word, he kicks at a tuft of dirt, setting off a cloud of brown dust.

"Please, I beg of you, tell me what's going on out there." My shrill tone is quite unbecoming, but I can't help it. "Speak the truth, even if I won't like it. Not knowing is worse torture."

He raises his head and looks me in the eye. "Lady President, it's been a shameful rout out there. There are no other words for it." He frowns. "We took a licking. Then everyone ran off like sheep chased by dogs."

My stomach bottoms out as I stand there in a stupor. Surely this man is delirious, overcome with exhaustion and the brutal heat. I don't want to believe him. I can't. There must be some other explanation.

French John fills the gap, brimming with his usual bravado. "Don't you worry, Madam Presidentess. No problem. I shall spike the cannon at the gate and lay a train of powder. If those brutes dare to open the front door, we will blow them into smithereens." He claps his hands together. "Boom, *voila!*"

His devotion to our cause brings the hint of a smile to my lips, something I thought impossible only a moment ago. This man is truly a child of the French Revolution. It's a brilliant idea, but I must refuse his gallant offer. My Quaker upbringing stands strong against violence, but I am so indebted to him, especially for his enthusiasm when I myself can muster none. It's a wonder that even he can feel so bold right now.

Two messengers arrive on horseback within their own swirling clouds of dust. As they gasp to catch some air, perspiration drips from their chins in round droplets. Between coughing fits, they spit out, "Ma'am, you must fly. The ruffians are at hand. It's not safe here for you anymore."

I don't flinch. "Thank you, gentlemen, but I shall wait for my husband." Raising my head, I then square my shoulders. "I'm determined that we go together. I fear great hostility toward him, even from our own countrymen. I must remain here to help him."

As the grandfather clock chimes three, a free black man gallops into view. A sour taste fills my mouth. Right now, I should be receiving guests and presiding over our savory dinner. Instead, I'm holding my breath as he waves his hat like a madman, shouting at the top of his lungs. Try as I might, I can't make out anything. He thunders right up to the doorstep with sweat shining through the dense layer of dirt on his face.

In a hoarse voice, he roars, "I've got a message for you, direct from President Madison! Clear out, clear out! General Armstrong has ordered a retreat! Retreat!" He jumps off his horse, bends over and sucks in some air with rasping breaths.

Those within earshot shout out, "Retreat!" Within

seconds, the soldiers in the park scatter like frightened children, splintering in every direction.

I am without words. I stand there, my feet rooted to the steps as my eyes bug out. This cannot be happening.

"Are you sure?" I finally sputter.

"Yes, ma'am! Never been so sure of anything in my whole life. You need to clear out now, Lady President. You ain't got a minute to lose! Those bloody Brits are right behind us, and they are looking for you special."

"But where's my husband?" I gasp. "I can't possibly leave without him."

"Ma'am, Madison bids you to fly! Leave now or you'll become their prisoner. And what a bind he'll be in then."

The man is right. I must flee. So, I elbow French John. "Find me a wagon."

He stares at me, dumbfounded by my outrageous demand. After all, wagons are more precious than rubies right now. But within an instant, he regains his unruffled demeanor. How I love him for it. "Yes, ma'am. Consider it done."

I turn to Paul. "Get Sukey, and bring the trunks down from the attic. Then pull the carriage around front."

With my lips pressed together in a grim line, I run back inside and race into Jemmy's study to gather his most important papers. Within minutes, Paul and Sukey deliver the chests. Paul dashes off to fetch the carriage, while Sukey and I fill every inch of the trunks with stacks of Jemmy's letters, ledgers, and journals. I even make sure to include his precious notes from the Constitutional Convention. Thankfully, he is just as diligent with his record-keeping as everything else.

Sukey wipes the glistening sweat from her forehead with the back of her hand and shakes it off. "What about your fancy dresses and all the turbans?"

I snap at her, my voice shrill. "Susan, some things are more important than clothes."

The poor girl winces, and bursts into tears. I never call her by her proper name.

"Sukey, please forgive me." My voice goes flat. "Our private property must be sacrificed. We have no room for them, and no time." I take a ragged breath. "Our garments can be replaced, but Mr. Madison's papers cannot."

We rearrange the papers to create some crevices. "Now let's collect all the treasures."

"But, Miss Dolley, the Brits are going to catch us!" Tears stream down her face. "We need to leave right away."

"Now, now, Sukey. We'll be fine. Just a few more things to do, and we'll be off."

By the time we push and tug the first chest to the front steps, a massive cart awaits us. The horses' ears flick back and forth as they snort, bracing themselves for the jolt of the cannon's next boom.

Wearing an impish smirk, French John bows low with a dramatic hand flourish. "As you requested, my dear Mrs. Madison."

I don't ask how he got it; I don't care. But if he hadn't, I would grab the Tunisian saber under my bed and commandeer one myself. What a headline that would make, "Beware of the Sword-Wielding Presidentess." Alas I have no time for daydreaming.

We fill the cart to the brim, stashing as many valuables as it can hold, including the new blue and gold Loughstaff China wrapped in linen napkins, my favorite silver tea service, and some serving pieces stuffed into vases. Thankfully I also remember to grab the bronze clock from Mrs. Adams. She left it for future generations, so it is my duty to preserve it for them. Unfortunately, that leaves no room for anything else, not even the precious scoops for serving my iced creams.

I order a wild-eyed Sukey to pull down the red curtains in the oval drawing room, making sure not to tear them. Then I drape them over the load, shielding Jemmy's invaluable papers from the swirling dust. My eyes dart over to the window. Try as I might to ignore the thick clouds advancing toward us, my mind runs wild with the worst possible scenarios. Is that our militia now in full retreat? Even worse, is Cockburn's vanguard arriving here to capture both the city and me? I've never been so hot in my life, yet I shiver like I've been plunged into a bath of ice cubes.

French John dispatches a servant to deliver Jemmy's documents to the Bank of Maryland. I pray with all my heart Cockburn's henchmen will not intercept it.

CHAPTER 19

RISING PANIC

T ime has run out. With my head down, I race through the dining room, grabbing all the silver flatware that my straining fists can hold. I thrust it deep into my pockets until they bulge like saddlebags. Then I look up and find myself standing face-to-face with the full likeness of General Washington.

I gasp. How can I leave this gallant portrait of the Father of Our Country behind to fall into Cockburn's clutches? It would become a heartbreaking trophy of war, a symbol of our demise, and damage our national pride, already so weak. Removing this massive painting high up on the wall would be no easy feat, though.

But I am torn.

I need to escape. I must leave this very second.

My heart pounds even harder, almost out of my chest, as I wrestle with my decision.

No, I must save it. I couldn't live with myself otherwise. I will sacrifice my stunning French gowns and exquisite drawing rooms, but not this.

In a shrill voice, I summon Paul, French John, and

Thomas, our gardener. "I won't allow the Brits to get their hands on this portrait! Oh, what fun they'd have mocking it in London!"

"But, Miss Dolley, it's attached to the wall, remember?" Paul stammers as sweat rolls down his face.

"Yes, of course, I do. But we don't have time to remove it, so just splinter the frame and cut the canvas out."

They blink at me in unison.

"I'm dead serious." I grit my teeth. "We have no choice. Go ahead!"

They stare at me, their mouths hanging open.

"Now!" I command.

Without a word, Thomas sprints out the back door, while French John scurries down the creaky steps to the cellar. Good heavens, the man is whistling. I don't know whether to admire or curse him, but I don't have the time to decide.

Our kind friend Mr. Carroll arrives to escort us back to his home in nearby Georgetown, Maryland. "Mrs. Madison, I beg you. We must depart for Belle Vue immediately. The rest of your party already awaits you in the carriage, and the British will arrive any moment. I can assure you of one thing. You'll make a far better prize for Cockburn than this portrait."

"Yes, yes, I know, Mr. Carroll." I'm tempted to growl at him but resist. "I want to leave here just as badly as you do, but we just can't leave it behind. It means too much to the American people." I don't mention the other major problem —we have nowhere to keep it. The cart has already departed for the Bank of Maryland.

After a few agonizing minutes, French John trots in, lugging a stepladder. Thomas returns, wielding a dusty axe that he wipes on his stained britches. John grabs it from him and races up the ladder. Thomas holds it steady while John pounds on the majestic frame, swinging one ferocious blow after another.

With a thunderous crack, the wood falls apart, sending jagged splinters flying all over the room. Some even land on my arms and shoulders, but I don't bother to brush them off. In a blur, John has transformed the stunning frame into a mangled pile of scraps. Thomas pulls out a pen knife and thrusts it at John who then cuts the portrait from the canvas. I hover over him, making annoying clucking sounds.

Like an envoy from God, our Quaker friend from New York, Mr. Barker, and his companion, Mr. DePeyster, arrive on my doorstep, offering to help in any way. I almost swoon with relief.

"Please take this, I'm most anxious to save it," I cry, balancing the huge canvas over my extended arms. "There is nothing more precious to America. Don't let it fall into the hands of the enemy. Its capture would make a brilliant finish for them." I take a deep breath and look them both in the eye. "But destroy it if you must."

"We are honored by your trust, Mrs. Madison," Mr. Barker replies. "I can assure you that we will do everything in our power to keep it safe."

Mr. DePeyster grabs an end of the portrait, curls the edge, and proceeds to roll it up.

"No! Stop!" bellows French John, startling us all.

"What in the world, John?" I snarl. Has he gone mad? I've never seen him so angry, and I now am quite furious with him as well.

"You mustn't do that!" he sputters, red in the face. "The paint will crack, and you'll ruin it!"

Pursing his lips, Mr. DePeyster releases the portrait, letting it unfurl.

As the two men head to the door with the canvas spread out between them, I take a heavy breath. The portrait, so treasured by our nation, now rests in their capable hands. I am ready.

"Let's give them your portrait as well," suggests French John.

"No, it's not important," I bark, shaking my head.

"Mrs. Madison, on this matter I must insist." He puts on a debonair smile, trots off to my parlor to fetch it, and then hands it to them.

Meanwhile I run like a fleeing burglar through the dining room one last time, grabbing our framed copy of the Declaration of Independence written by Mr. Jefferson. With my other hand, I grab a few tiny treasures and rush out the front door. Since my hands are too full to shut it behind me, I grimace and circle back. Then I scold myself. How ridiculous to even bother closing the door. It doesn't matter anymore.

My frantic eyes land on the ornate knob, our only source of elegance when we first moved in. "Please help me," I shriek up to Paul in the driver's box with the reins already taut in his hands. "I can't leave the doorknob behind. We must take it with us!"

Next to him, Sukey puts her head in her hands, moaning, "Miss Dolley, if we don't go now, they're going to get us!"

Paul jumps down with a thud, stirring up yet more dust. He sprints over and tinkers with the knob as sweat drips from his chin. After a several long minutes, he breaks it apart and slides the pieces into his pockets. He puts his fist through the empty round hole, waits for me to walk out, and then pulls it shut behind us. Locking the door is no longer an option.

Grabbing my skirt, I all but leap into the carriage, landing next to Anna. I allow myself to take one last look over my shoulder. French John stands on the front steps, saluting my carriage.

"God save Queen Dolley!" squawks an eerily familiar voice.

With a start, I jump back out, forgetting my rheumatism. There is my beloved pet, perched on John's shoulder. Why, I forgot all about my poor bird! "Polly! What on Earth shall I do with you?" I can't leave her here. Lord knows what they would do to her, but she certainly can't come with us either.

"No worries, I'll take her under my wing." French John flaps his arm. "She'll be just fine. My children will love her." He smirks. "She can entertain us while we cower in the cellar."

"But what if they burn down the entire city?" I cry, far from convinced.

"So, you're more worried about your bird than your beloved Master of Ceremonies and his family?" He winks.

I glare at him. I'm in no mood for humor, not even his.

He clears his throat. "Well, how about the Octagon House then? Colonel Tahoe turned it over to the French Embassy, so the Brits won't dare burn it. They sure don't want to risk stirring up another war with France."

I lock eyes with him and refuse to blink.

"I'll walk her over there myself, right after you leave," he declares.

I continue to stare at him.

"*Grace a dieu*, I promise you, Mrs. Madison. But now you must go, before you end up like Marie Antoinette. Trust me, it was not a pretty sight."

I put my hands on my hips, fighting my natural impulse to stay and face those brutes myself. However, I must leave the Great Castle now or our invaders will fill the road and trap me here. Then they'll parade me through the streets of London in irons.

If only I could have a cannon in every window and bombard our evil enemy! But who would put them there?

And who would stay to fire them? I must escape before it's too late! Perhaps it already is. They may very well apprehend us on our way to Georgetown. I grit my teeth. We will soon find out.

"I wish someone could stay here and report on their every move," I mutter under my breath.

French John's eyes widen for a split second. I swear there's a glimmer of fear.

"Not you, John. They'd grab you in an instant. It would have to be someone else, someone they would never notice... But that's impossible. Anyone left lurking around the city would draw suspicion."

"I can do it, Miss Dolley," says a resolute voice behind me.

Putting a hand to my chest, I whirl around and stare up at Paul in the driver's box. "My dear boy, oh no. It's much too dangerous for you."

"But they'd won't pay me any mind, ma'am. I'd be just a slave child wandering the streets."

I pause. After all, he does make an excellent point. "But you can't stay here. We need you to drive the carriage."

"I can drive you folks wherever you need to go, Miz Madison," Thomas the gardener pipes up. "I've been driving a wagon since I was a young'un."

Raising my eyebrows, I look over at Anna and French John. They nod our heads in unison.

"Paul, we've got a shed out back for you," French John offers.

"Well, it's decided then," I announce. "Thank you, Paul. This is so very brave of you."

With a shy smile, he drops the reins and hops down.

"Paul, you keep safe now!" shrieks Sukey, poking her head out the open door.

"Don't you go worrying, sister Sukey." He smiles over at

her. "They won't even notice me spying on them. I'll see you soon."

Dong. The grandfather clock strikes the half-hour. Goodness gracious, it is 3:30.

Thomas mounts the driver's box, and I climb back into the crowded coach. At long last, we pull away from my beloved home.

Rounding the corner onto Pennsylvania Avenue, anguish fills my heart. "Madison comes not; may God protect him!" I blurt out, tormented by a moment of weakness.

Then I push my head out the tiny window and crane my neck in both directions. I'm frantic to catch a glimpse of my husband, praying he will appear any second. Why isn't he back yet? Where could he be? I pray the enemy didn't capture him. I can't bear that possibility. I just can't. Tears roll down my face in a torrential downpour, turning everything into a blurry fog.

"Come here, sister." Anna rubs my drenched back and then smooths back the stray wisps of wet hair from my face. Wrapping her moist arm around my shoulder, she pulls me toward her, tucking my head into the soft curve of her shoulder. How I savor this sticky embrace. Our roles have reversed. For so many years I raised her as my sister-daughter, and now she is rescuing me from the brink of insanity.

I am overcome with hacking sobs. Alarmed, the boys drop their pewter toy soldiers and burst into tears themselves, even the manly James Madison Cutts. Little Dolley wails for her beloved dollhouse that we had to leave behind for those brutes to destroy. I still can't stop my breakdown, though.

"I feel so wretched for leaving without Jemmy," I confess to Anna. My chest heaves, and I can hardly speak through my outpouring of tears. It's amazing my body has any liquid left after soaking through my dresses for days on end. "He offered for me to go early, but I told him I'd wait. I broke my promise."

She hugs me close to her bulging stomach. I can even feel her baby kicking. "Sister, we had to go before they caught us. Remember, he sent a messenger telling you to leave. Listen to me, sister, listen. That means he's safe. He's not a prisoner. He'll find us down the road just as soon as he can. I promise you, he will."

For the sake of the distraught children, I finally regain my composure and stare out the window. The appalling scenario is the stuff of nightmares. Torn suitcases, mangled wheels, and broken-down wagons lay abandoned in the most haphazard fashion. Some even block the road, hindering our delayed departure. The stark evidence of our citizens' unbridled terror shames me. In their haste to flee the capital, our countrymen were desperate enough to sacrifice anything and everything. Despite our best intentions, we failed them in the worst way imaginable.

A well-loved doll lies abandoned in the middle of the road, her happy smile stitched in wide loops with bright red yarn. Oh, the poor baby was no doubt thrown overboard in the chaos. Lines of dirt crisscross her cloth body from the countless wheels that have run over her during the disorderly flight from Washington City. Her little owner must be broken-hearted without her precious dolly. I let out a sob for yet another innocent victim of this catastrophe, altogether too many to count.

Terrifying thoughts run through my mind. How did we reach such a devastating level of anguish? What could Jemmy have done to prevent the enemy from reaching our doorstep? Will America ever be the same country again? God help us, will America still *be* a country after this atrocity? Perhaps we've ruined it once and for all, and our destiny is to become

British subjects once again. I've never seen such a sorry spectacle.

We are among the last caravans leaving Washington City. I am numb from head to toe. It's all I can do to nod. Am I still alive or trapped in a nightmare that will never end? No, this is far worse. This is real.

A troubling curtain of quiet has fallen over the abandoned city, a stark contrast to the utter pandemonium just an hour ago. It's downright eerie. "Well, at least the roads are empty now, so we can make our way much faster," Anna mutters, squeezing my hand. We are bound together by slippery sweat mixed with tears.

Neither of us dares to mention our fear of immediate apprehension. After all, we are on the open road, exposed without a single guard. The British could intercept our wagon without any effort and make us their prisoners, including my adorable niece and nephews. Of course, the walls of the President's House offered much more protection, but it is their main target. We had to escape before it became our jail, funeral pyre, and tomb. Hopefully we still have enough time to slip away before they lay waste to our capital city, destroying it before our elaborate plans are even finished.

CHAPTER 20
ON THE RUN
AUGUST 24, 1814, AT FOUR O'CLOCK

As we trot down the dusty road toward Mr. Carrol's brick mansion on Q Street in Georgetown, I stare out the window, cowering at each bend in the road. Twice I shriek, convinced the British are marching around the corner, but thankfully my mind is seeing things. Alas, the beastly heat, frayed nerves, and utter exhaustion have gotten the best of me. I force myself to sit back and comfort the terrified children. Finally noticing the sharp splinters from the frame still on my shoulders, I brush them off.

At long last, we arrive at the stately Belle Vue. Much to my irritation, though, Mr. Carroll insists on peeking behind every last bush before letting us exit the carriage. He's convinced Cockburn and his cohorts lie in wait, ready to spring out at us any second. Once he finally assures himself of our safety, he hurries us inside, looking over his shoulder the whole time.

We wait in anxious silence for Jemmy, each minute crawling by like a century. At long last, a breathless messenger arrives with a few snippets of news. Praise the Lord above! After leaving the battlefield, Jemmy went by the President's

House, hoping to find me still there despite his order to leave.

In the interim, our panic-stricken troops have dispersed in every direction, clogging the roads throughout the city. Alas, now Jemmy is unable to make his way over to us in Georgetown. How my heart hurts. He will take Mason's Ferry across the Potomac into Virginia. God willing, he will then meet us at Wiley's Tavern in Great Falls.

I'm crushed Jemmy can't get here, but I force myself to count my blessings. Most important, he is safe, at least for now. I grit my teeth. After all, this nightmare is just beginning. I must persevere without him, hoping to make him and my countrymen proud.

Just after five, we leave Mr. Carroll and the safety of his home behind us. Now we are officially evacuees, too. Unfortunately, since the entire militia has disintegrated, meandering soldiers now crowd the roads around us as well. Our progress is painfully slow, taking us hours to go just a few miles.

At long last, we trot across the Potomac at Little Falls Bridge. Normally its loose planks worry me, but I want to kneel and kiss each one for getting us to the other side. Thank goodness the children are fast asleep, but Anna and I manage a tiny cheer. Virginia has always been the true home of my heart, but I've never experienced any greater relief than rolling onto its hallowed ground right now. I release a ragged sigh, elated that a river separates me from bloody Cockburn and his evil marauders.

As the sun sets, a deafening blast comes from Washington City behind us. Anna and I lock wide eyes and shake our heads. Of course, we have no idea what just happened, but it cannot be good. Soon the sun sets on on us like a giant candle blown out. Soft golden clouds float above us, basking in the glow of the pale moon. It's a dream-like setting for the worst night of my life. Even though we are now in the beloved haven of Virginia, we are still not safe. I am wary of those countrymen who are furious at Jemmy for our wartime debacles.

I would love nothing more than to reach our original meeting place at Wiley's Tavern. However, traveling that extra distance through the darkness worries me. It may not be wise, especially with pregnant Anna and her little ones in tow. Goodness knows what kind of angry mob we could encounter along the route. We didn't go to such great lengths to escape those British savages only to endure harassment or worse from our fellow Americans.

CHAPTER 21

THE WORLD ON FIRE

NIGHT OF AUGUST 24, 1814

"D on't take the next turn for Wiley's Tavern," I direct Thomas in a hoarse voice. "Let's keep heading south to Rokeby Farm. It's up on a hill, not too far from here. I know Matilda Lee Love will take us in."

Indeed, just a few minutes later, my friend greets us on her doorstep with hearty hugs for every member of our long-faced group, insisting we stay the night. Before taking another breath, I accept her generous offer. After all, we have no other safe option.

As we enter the doorway, a houseful of disheveled women and children stares at me in awkward silence. I want to shrink into the wall, but to my relief, they break into a polite round of applause.

I muster a wan smile, a foreign feeling after the traumatic events of the past few days. We inch our way into the parlor while Matilda sends a servant to prepare emergency accommodations for my miserable entourage.

"Pray tell, where is President Madison tonight?" asks a concerned woman. "I so desperately hope for his well-being."

"I can assure you the president is quite safe. I wish to tell you more, but I'm sworn to secrecy." I feign an air of confidence, as if we are following some ingenious master plan. Unfortunately, the truth is too frightening to admit. I have no more idea than she does where he is right now.

As the cook bustles through the crowd carrying a stack of plates, Matilda squeezes my arm. "Dolley, may we please get you some coffee? You must be parched after such a long journey."

I pause, noticing all of a sudden that my tongue is sticking to the roof of my mouth. "Why, thank you so much, Matilda. That would be lovely."

The cook wheels around, looks me in the eye, and glares. "I ain't in no hurry to get no coffee for the likes of her." She raises her chin at me. "Mr. Madison and that Mr. Armstrong done sold our country to the British."

Pursing her lips into a grim line, Matilda chases her into the kitchen. A few minutes later, the cook returns with a steaming cup. Making no effort to hide her scowl, she pushes it into my hands, but I don't dare take a sip.

I have no idea of the time, but it's quite late. Anna feeds her bleary-eyed children some bread and cheese, and Sukey helps settle them into bed. Then Matilda serves us a hearty stew with a glass of Madeira. I am so grateful for this simple yet savory meal. Thankfully little did I know that at the same time, Cockburn and his henchmen were inside the President's House, celebrating their seamless victory. Indeed, they were toasting with our crystal goblets, drinking our fine chilled wine, and stuffing themselves with Jemmy's favorite dinner. How naïve I was. A wave of fatigue washes over me, so I gulp down my food without tasting it, desperate to escape to my room.

Once I find myself alone, I fling myself onto the bed and

sob into my pillow. I hope no one can overhear, but I can't hold back my tears a minute longer.

Anna throws open the door and stands aghast in the doorway. "Sister, for the love of God, look what's happened!" she screams.

Drying my eyes with the back of my hands, I race over to the window to yank back the curtains. She beats me to it, though, revealing the most appalling sight of my life.

"God help us, Washington City is on fire!" I shout at the top of my lungs, no longer caring who can hear me. Pulling my fists to my mouth, I pray Jemmy made it out alive.

A towering inferno burns in front of me, filling the skyline. It's our glorious Capitol, the first public building that the enemy would encounter coming down Maryland Avenue from Bladensburg. The massive columns of flames and smoke have jagged peaks of orange and red. They shift up and down like they are alive, bursting with sparks, making the disastrous scene even more eerie.

Soon everyone at Rokeby crowds around the front windows, yelling and weeping, too. Thankfully Sukey and the children are all so exhausted that they sleep right through the pandemonium. I am so grateful God shows them such mercy, sparing them from witnessing the fires of Hell that have overtaken their city. How those memories would scar their tiny souls. My horror only grows as I realize the blaze must include our Library of Congress with its 3,000 rare volumes as well as the Supreme Court. After all, they're all housed within the Capitol.

Soon a new flame ignites and grows in fury on the ghastly horizon. I pray it's not the President's House, but I am resigned to it, the subject of so many threats. Within another hour, a third mammoth bonfire lights up the sky with dancing flames. This must be either the Treasury, the State Department or both. My depth of my sorrow knows no bounds.

When I'm too spent to cry anymore, I plunk down into a chair by the open window, hoping the slight breeze will air out my sorrows. Instead, the smell of burning wood and smoke fills my nostrils. Where is Jemmy? Did he make it all the way to Wiley's Tavern? How I long for him to knock on the door and hold me in a sweet embrace while I wail on his shoulder.

Every time I look out on the ominous horizon, I must stifle a shriek. A huge red glow fills the space where our capital city stood just a few hours ago. There is no mistaking the gigantic balls of fire and the glowing sparks mounting higher, shooting toward the sky. They redden the heavens and outshine the moon. I am terrified the fire will spread even further since the ground is so parched after three weeks without rain.

I don't know why this sea of soaring flames shocks me so. Cockburn has been threatening this devastation for the past year. He wouldn't balk upon entering our capital and finding it ripe for ravaging. In fact, he'd probably drool like a starving wolf stumbling on a flock of newborn lambs. Bile rises in my throat as I imagine his glee, but I push it back down. He is not worth my vomit.

Anna knocks on my door and tiptoes in. "I'm back to keep you company, sister."

"Thank you, I can't bear being alone with my torturous thoughts for another moment." Tears roll down my cheeks. "I'm so terribly worried about Jemmy. I have no idea where he is and no way to find him. He could be anywhere out there, lost or wounded or..." I sweep my arm and let it fall, slapping my side.

"Jemmy is a shrewd man, even during the worst of circumstances," she reassures me, curling her arm around my shoulder. "I have no doubt he made it across at Mason's Ferry without a hitch. Then he probably stayed somewhere nearby, just like us. We'll find him tomorrow. Let's keep faith. Now let me tuck you in, just as you did for me so many years."

"Thank you, sister," I mumble as she leads me into bed. "What would I ever do without you?"

"Let's pray you never have to find out." She smooths back my disheveled hair and kisses my forehead.

CHAPTER 22
THE STORM THAT SAVES
WASHINGTON CITY
AUGUST 25, 1814

I have a fitful sleep, dreaming Cockburn and his hateful Redcoats track me down and set Rokeby Farm afire, too. Early the next morning, I awake in a coughing fit with acrid smoke filling the room. I make my way through the thick gray haze to the window. To my horror, massive fires still burn tall over Washington City, even dominating the rising sun. I stand there as if glued to the floor, stupefied. I could gape at this heinous view forever and never comprehend the depths of this calamity.

As we set off for Wiley's Tavern, the wind blows and soon develops into powerful gusts. The sky turns black, lined with ferocious clouds. The horses become skittish in the sudden darkness, so Thomas pulls in the reins. Thankfully we reach our destination before the impending storm can escalate any further.

Jemmy is not there; and there's no message from him waiting for us either. Alas, my hopes are dashed again. Sweet Anna approaches the tavern-keeper's wife amidst an ornery crowd of displaced women, so I can slip upstairs. As the wind turns into a full-fledged gale, apples fly from the trees and pound against the house in loud sporadic thuds. I am too tired even to cry, so I lie down and close my eyes, savoring the solitude.

A commotion erupts downstairs and grows louder. "Miss Madison!" the tavern-keeper's wife yells up the stairs.

Shaken, I sit up and stare at the door, wondering if I misheard. Surely she would not address me in such an inhospitable fashion. Perhaps the British have tracked me down here, and she is trying to warn me.

"Miss Madison, if that's you," she bellows, "come down here right now, and go out!"

I gasp at this appalling treatment. Even the Society of Friends was more humane when they cast me out for marrying Jemmy.

"My husband fought in the Revolution, and your husband has got him out there fighting again as an old man," she shouts. "Damn you, you shan't stay in my house, so get out!"

To my eternal embarrassment, the other women join in, chanting, "Get out! Get out! Get out!" while clapping in unison. I slap a hand to my mouth as their ugliness stings my soul. In all my years, I've never suffered such mistreatment, especially from fellow Americans. One thing is certain; this war has brought out the best in some and the worst in others. I want so much to lecture them on their traitorous ways, but I refuse to stoop to their base level.

Instead, I jump to my feet. With my shoulders thrown back and head held high, I march down the stairs. My heart aches as my sister-daughter pleads with the tavern-keeper's wife. "Madam, I'm so sorry your husband is out there. I pray he is safe and thank you for his service. Please let us stay, at least through the downpour. President Madison plans to meet us here, and we have no other way to reach him."

Without a word, I walk straight out the door into the violent gale. Although the sun has not set, it is black as midnight outside. Lightning bolts illuminate the sky, flashing down from the angry clouds all the way down to the ground. Majestic oak trees topple over like twigs, thankfully not landing on the tavern. Out in the barn, the dogs howl, horses whinny, and hogs scream.

In minutes, the wind whips up into the full-blown frenzy of a hurricane. Suddenly the sky opens up, and a massive deluge of water beats down on me. Deafening peals of thunder crash all around me. I let it wash over me, unable to fight anymore. I am spent. In a hoarse voice, I look up to the raging heavens and declare, "Dear God, please take me now."

Suddenly the mistress of the tavern throws open the door and shouts at me. I can barely hear her above the storm's fury, so she beckons me over to her, shrieking, "Miss Madison! You can stay, but only because of the gales. I want you out tomorrow. You hear me?"

"Yes, ma'am," I reply, summoning every remaining shred of dignity in my soul. "Thank you, and I'm sincerely sorry for your troubles." Soaked to my skin, I walk back inside and trudge upstairs where I receive a bear hug from Anna. By now, the flying apples from the orchard have shattered several windows, allowing the drenching rain and wind to swirl around the tavern.

Just as the worst of it passes, several horses gallop up the road and stop in front of the tavern. I sprint over to the window like Cockburn himself is chasing me. When I recognize the new arrivals, I let out a long exhale and clutch my hands to my heart.

Jemmy is here, at long last!

Hallelujah!

CHAPTER 23

REUNION WITH JEMMY

Jemmy's footsteps already pound on the stairs as I throw open my door. He races in and embraces me, pressing so hard against me I can't breathe. His clothes are sopping wet, but I wouldn't have it any other way. I've never known such joy in my life as this moment. After thirty-six hours of searching for each other, we are finally together again.

"My dearest, how I've dreamed of this," he exclaims with a kiss. "It's been the worst kind of hide-and-seek, my apologies. By the time we got over the bridge last night, it was already dark, so we stopped at the first place that we could find, Salona."

"We made it just a bit further to Rokeby Farm," I murmur.

Lowering his voice, he whispers into my unkempt hair, "Are you all right? I've been thinking of you every second."

"Yes, I'm fine." My voice cracks as we sit on the bed arm in arm. "How are you? I've been so terribly worried." I rest my head on his shoulder.

"I'm fine, too, thank God," he mumbles. But we know

that's not true, none of it. I'm not fine, and neither is he. We will never be fine again.

"Oh, Jemmy, it looked like the world was on fire." I turn to look at him. "I've never seen anything like it."

"Yes, our entire world was in flames." His bloodshot eyes grow misty. "Everything we worked so hard to build since the Revolution turned to smoke and ashes right in front of our eyes." He shrugs as if trying to shake off the enormity of this calamity. "But at least we weren't there to witness the Union Jack flying over Washington City. I just couldn't bear it."

"I can hardly even handle the thought. What a ferocious storm, Jemmy. But it put out the fires, though, thanks be to God. How much worse they would've been without it. I was so afraid the flames would spread and destroy every house in the city."

"Jefferson said it would be a mere matter of marching for us to take Canada." His voice turns bitter. "Instead, it ended up being a mere matter of marching for those scoundrels to occupy Washington City. But I can't dwell on it, or the irony will drive me mad."

As we gaze at the fiery skyline of our national home, I cling to him. I have so much to tell him, yet nothing at all. I am numb.

Jemmy sinks back on my unmade bed and stares up at the ceiling. I join him, interlacing my hand with his. "When we first crossed over the bridge into Bladensburg, we almost blundered right into the Brits," he confides in a faraway voice. "For the life of me, I can't decide who's more incompetent, Winder or Armstrong."

I sigh. How could these fools let such a thing happen?

"Don't worry, my dear." He looks over at me and manages a feeble smile. "Then I took your advice and withdrew to the rear. After all, I'm not much good as president if I'm a prisoner of war."

"Yes, we can't afford to lose our president!" I force down a lump in my throat. "Thank God you got your wits about you and weren't caught up in the middle of it."

"That was my first time on a battlefield, and it was sobering," Jemmy confesses in a hoarse voice. "There's nothing glorious about war." He coughs into his balled-up fist. "For such a quick battle, I've never witnessed such horrors."

I squeeze my eyes shut, but I still want to know more. "Tell me, Jemmy. What happened out there?"

"First they sent off a hailstorm of cannonballs and charged at us. Then they launched their new Congreve rockets, the same ones they used to defeat Napoleon." He waves his hands in the air. "They flew right over our heads, whooshing in this massive arc."

"Dearest, I've never been so terrified in all my life." He raises my hand and kisses it. "They were loaded with gunpowder and left a fiery trail in the sky behind them. Oh, they made such a horrible shrieking sound. It still haunts me and probably always will." Despite the heat, he shivers.

"Our terrified militia men dropped their weapons and fled in every direction, and then the reinforcements did the same." His shoulders sag. "The Brits have already dubbed it the Bladensburg Races. Our troops sprinted away so fast that it was like a horse race, and they say I was their tiny jockey." He shakes his head, trying make the memory disappear. "But to me, they looked more like a terrified flock of chickens chased by wolves. I'm not sure which is worse."

"How humiliating," I murmur.

"It was a total disaster." He shakes his head. "We soon realized the rockets were wildly inaccurate, but by then it was much too late. The damage was done."

"Absolutely horrible." I blink several times, trying to process it all.

"I never would've believed the difference between regular

troops like the Brits and our pathetic militia if I hadn't seen it with my own eyes." He shrugs. "There is no comparison."

"But didn't you and Mr. Jefferson oppose having a standing national army?" I ask, curious.

"Yes, we did." He frowns. "We were afraid of government tyranny, but now I realize how wrong we were. The militia had no decent training and totally panicked."

"Well, we all learn from our experiences, don't we?" I wedge my arm behind his neck and kiss him on the cheek.

"Then the canons fired off even more deafening rolls of thunder. There were huge holes everywhere, like giant pockmarks all over the field."

"I can't imagine the noise." I cringe. "Even I could hear the roaring from miles away."

"But through it all, the crossfire of muskets never stopped. Tiny pieces of white cartridge paper covered the entire field." His eyes take on a faraway look. "It reminded me of the cotton fields at Montpelier, only bodies lay strewn everywhere, too."

"The smell was dreadful." He wrinkles his nose. "The gunpowder reeked of rotten eggs and let off a thick smoke. A dense fog hung over the field, stinging my eyes and throat."

I sigh. Suddenly my eyes and throat tingle a bit as well.

"Soon that was like perfume in comparison. The battlefield also stank of blood, vomit, urine, and feces. I bet the stench is still overpowering from a mile away, especially with those dead bodies decomposing in this unbearable heat. I wonder if that God-forsaken odor will ever leave my nostrils."

He closes his eyes. "Sixty of our men dropped right in their tracks."

"Dropped dead? From what?" I'm incredulous.

"Heatstroke." His chin trembles. "They spent all day baking in their woolen uniforms and thick leather helmets."

"Goodness gracious, what a travesty!"

"Yes, indeed, but I pitied the wounded the most of all. They lost control of their bodies right away." He draws in a big breath and then exhales. "When a cannonball blew off a leg or a bayonet sliced open a stomach, those soldiers didn't die in silence. Oh, their screams were shrill enough to carry over the din of battle, calling out for their mothers, for a sip of water. I've never heard such ghastly sounds." Tears roll down his cheeks. "I wanted to stay and help every single one of them."

I nod, squeezing his hand as he collects himself.

"God help those poor soldiers who suffered through those grisly amputations. I've never seen anything so horrific in my entire life. The surgeon would pull his bone saw back and forth, standing in blood to his ankles. Such a hideous noise. I nearly retched, and I only stopped there for a moment." He grimaces. "A bone saw! Even the words pain me. No wonder they called him Dr. Sawbones. Their poor friends had to restrain them, using all their might. Let me tell you, there's no better friends in the entire world."

My eyes fill to the brim.

"Those sorry souls had nothing to ease their agony, just a bit of shoe leather to bite on. Woe to them, and such woe I've never seen."

I let my tears flow. They stream down the sides of my face, wetting my hair and trickling into my ears. I want to tell him to stop, but he needs to talk.

"Body parts were stacked in huge piles outside the hospital tent. But the nightmare was only just beginning. They expected many infections would set in within a few days." He shakes his head. "Being dead is much easier."

He glances over at me, as if remembering where he is. "Darling, did you hear those deafening booms yesterday around sunset?"

"Yes, what on Earth *were* they? Anna and I were horrified. They even woke the children from their naps."

"It was us." He presses his lips together and takes a deep swallow. "We blew up the Navy Yard so the Brits couldn't seize it."

"Oh, my goodness!" I exclaim, stunned.

"Remember our two new warships, the USS *Columbia* and the *Argus*?" His tone is bitter.

"Of course! They're the pride of the Navy and Washington City. We're supposed to launch them in a couple of weeks." I hold my breath, praying they are safe.

"Well, not anymore. They're now smoking carcasses, along with the sawmill and all the timber." He waves his hand in the air. "Gone, poof!"

I stare at him, dumbfounded, as we sit in shocked silence. Finally I speak up. "Jemmy, another ghastly explosion went off this afternoon. Didn't you hear it? It came from somewhere in Washington City."

He nods, his eyes wide. "Yes, I'm sure even the dead heard it. But I still have no idea what fresh catastrophe that was."

Beyond words, we cling to each other and weep.

"Dearest, I can't stay much longer," he whispers.

"Oh no! Why not?" I stare at him, aghast. I thought our painful separation was finally over, once and for all.

"There are ugly rumors." Jemmy takes a raggedy breath. "One is that the Brits are moving into Virginia to capture me."

"Dear God, no!" Will this nightmare never end?

"And our spies report that Cockburn has been harassing citizens in the street, asking, 'Where'd the little president go? If you can tell me, I promise a handsome reward.'"

"That swine!" I all but growl.

"So, I must stay on the move." He grimaces. "What if word gets out that I'm here, and he captures us both?"

My stomach plummets. I have no words to respond.

With both of us in tears again, he departs around midnight, heading north to join the remnants of our pitiful army up in Brookeville, Maryland. I'm terrified for his safety but so thankful for these few hours together, though they passed like seconds. We make a plan to meet at Anna's house on F Street as soon as it is safe, if ever.

IN THE MORNING, ANNA AND I RETREAT SOUTHEAST TO THE home of our friend Colonel Minor and wait there for an update. We hold our breath whenever a wagon rumbles down the lane, wondering who makes their arrival. After all, it could be just a friendly courier—or Cockburn himself arriving with his henchmen to capture us. Exhausted and unnerved, we gather the children and get on our knees to pray that the British abandon Washington City. But why in the world would they decide to leave? After all, there's no one left there to throw them out.

After a sleepless night at Minor's Hill, another massive blast sounds off from the south, setting off jarring vibrations. Soon we receive yet more calamitous news. When the British fleet headed up the Potomac, the Commander of Fort Warburton lost his nerve. Without firing a single shot in defense of the fort, he blew up the entire compound and withdrew, leaving the river wide open for the enemy to advance. The city of Alexandria now lay unprotected just a few miles upriver, a prime target for plundering.

Horrible news spreads that Alexandria capitulated without a word of protest even before the British arrived. Yes, this is the same Alexandria near Mount Vernon where General Washington once attended church. How mortifying. They agreed to surrender their ships, armaments, tobacco, flour, cotton, and drink, as well as all merchandise stored in their warehouses. The only concession by the bullying British was a promise not to destroy any homes. However, even that was conditioned upon meeting no resistance when they entered the city.

"They should let their city be burned rather than submit to such humiliating terms!" I fume to Anna. "They are traitors to America!"

Later on, the Mayor of Georgetown crumbles as well, that spineless fool. I am appalled that he even grovels to Cockburn and offers him a white flag. Rumors swirl of Cockburn's obnoxious announcement, "Since your president won't protect you, I will. I'll take better care of you than Jemmy did. Never fear, you will be safer under my administration than his."

To my overwhelming relief, that evening I finally receive a message from Jemmy, scrawled on a dirty scrap of paper.

Dearest,

Our invaders left last night after the 8 o'clock curfew in complete silence, under the cover of darkness. That ferocious storm spooked them—and so did a gruesome explosion while raiding our ammo depot at Greenleaf's Point. Many were blown to bits with countless others buried alive. My sources say the carnage was a thousand times more distressing than the battle. I cannot even imagine the suffering, but God only knows what mayhem they plan next. However, it appears safe to return now, so I shall set off immediately. I ask you to do the same, but please come in disguise. How I look forward to being with you, hoping never to part again.

J

. . .

MY HEART SOARS. AT LONG LAST, THEY ARE GONE AND SO much sooner than expected! Reading it aloud to Anna, I gloat, "How providential! The fury of that storm, and now this horrific explosion. I must admit my delight that God unleashed his wrath on those evil brutes."

Within seconds, though, my euphoria evaporates. Serious doubts flood my mind about our security back in Washington City. At this point I don't feel safe anywhere. However, despite everything that has gone wrong, I still trust Jemmy's judgment above anyone else's, even my own. I would follow him anywhere.

CHAPTER 24
BACK TO THE ASHES
AUGUST 28, 1814

By Sunday, four days after the torching of Washington City's public buildings, the shell-shocked residents need to see me back there amongst them. At Jemmy's request, I masquerade as a dowdy country matron. After the tragic event of the past few days, this transition doesn't bother me a bit. It's only clothing after all.

Over a dingy dress made of homespun, I cinch a soiled apron around my waist and place a shabby gray shawl around my shoulders. Instead of my trademark turban with its exotic feathers, I don a faded brown sunbonnet with an extra wide brim. Thankfully it succeeds in covering most of my face. Then I tuck every last tendril of my curly black hair underneath to avoid recognition. Since my favorite embroidered slippers are now a foul mud color, they blend right in with my humble outfit.

An eerie stillness fills the air. The silence is so loud it is deafening. I dread going back to Washington City with every fiber of my being, but it's crucial to raise morale. I mustn't appear afraid, although I quake at the thought. After all, a significant threat still lingers. Those nefarious marauders could return any moment, so our decision to return is a dangerous gamble. Jemmy and I have eluded them so far, but that is no guarantee. They could still catch us and accomplish their ultimate goal.

Indeed, our national nightmare is far from over. In fact, I fear this could be just the beginning. After all, Cockburn has made due on every other threat. He proved that blasted Armstrong completely wrong, just as we suspected all along. As much as I adore Jemmy, he's an even bigger fool for failing to fire him months ago. As a result, the sacred buildings of Washington City are now scorched earth.

With one glance at the raging Potomac, my eyes bug out. It's far wider than I've ever seen it, as lawless as our nation's capital. The dirty water churns like a maelstrom far higher than its normal banks. Foamy white caps rise up and crest as big sticks, logs, and debris race down, propelled by the ferocious current. The river surges with the savagery of a wild animal escaped from captivity.

Since the British destroyed the bridges, my bedraggled entourage and I must find another way to cross these angry waters, leaving our carriage behind. Spotting a long queue for a flimsy boat, we wait in line for hours. When we finally make it to the head of line, Anna approaches the disheveled owner, talking in a hushed tone. Finally, she confesses that we don't have any money.

"This ain't no free ride," he bellows, leaning into her. "No, ma'am!"

She steps forward and whispers into his ear, gesturing back to me.

"You not foolin' me," he scoffs, pointing at me. "That ain't no Lady President over there. You go find yourself another boat."

Sweet Anna begs him to calm down, but his outrage only escalates. "If you ain't got money, you go swim across for all I care."

Pursing my lips, I stalk over to him. Ripping off my sunbonnet, I stare him down.

"Come along then, Lady President," he stammers, flushing like an overripe tomato.

Of course, I'm relieved to secure our passage. However, I'm equally aghast at the pathetic state of our transport. We are entrusting our lives to it since none of us know how to swim. Should this leaky device give out, the raging river would sweep us all away within seconds. My water-logged dress, alone, would drag me down to its murky depths.

Despite the oppressive humidity, I shiver. I can't endure this living nightmare much longer. Perhaps I'll go to bed and stay there until I die, just like Father. Now I better understand his black moods and how he found it impossible to go on. Some burdens are just too much to bear.

Covering my eyes, I fight the instinct to run away. I remind myself of my duty to my countrymen. Plus, I must set an example for my whimpering niece and nephews. Looking away from Sukey's teary eyes and quivering lips, I force myself to step onto the shaky boat, first with one hesitant foot and then the other. I must return to Washington City right away and show my dedication remains steadfast, that I haven't faltered, not even for an instant. Yet I have, and for much longer than that. I must appear unafraid, yet I am terrified to the core of my soul. I need to show steely resolve, but I'd rather curl up into a ball and sob until no tears remain.

Once our pitiful crew finally gets onboard and crosses the Potomac, the storm's vast destruction is evident right away. The shacks that once lined the river banks have been decimated. They are now sodden piles of shredded planks. But nothing could ever prepare me for the utter devastation awaiting us in our conquered national capital. The acrid smell of smoke hangs heavy in the air, choking us. People scuttle about like street urchins, looking stunned and devastated. I feel the same. Everyone is still a refugee, even in their own city. There is no escaping the pain as lawlessness abounds.

Even worse, in their haste to depart, the British abandoned the dead and wounded, leaving them right where they dropped. Naked corpses lie strewn like human trash, stripped by rampant looters. Dead horses abound in various twisted contortions, left to rot. Oh, the stench is nauseating. Between their heartbreaking howls, the little ones vomit what little is left in their tiny stomachs. I fight the urge to retch into the streams of mud, too.

While Anna secures a wagon for us, I glance downriver toward Alexandria. Much to my horror, the entire British fleet has just arrived and sails into the harbor in its full glory. The Union Jack waves merrily from the top of the mast on every ship.

Despite the rampant humidity, chills run down my spine. I let out a screech and clap my hand to my mouth. Rage consumes me as I witness the people of Alexandria do nothing to protect their city.

"How can they just sit back and welcome those robbers?" I rage to Anna.

"They don't deserve to call themselves Americans," she agrees.

"I bet they'll return to Washington City." Gritting my teeth, I brace myself for more debauchery. "Why wouldn't they? There's no one left to stop them."

Thankfully I don't find out about Alexandria's final act of cowardice until later. This one borders on treason. Even after the British departed and sailed twenty miles downstream, those sniveling fools still refused to raise our flag. They only hoisted it when an American naval officer threatened to shell the city if they didn't. What pathetic rubbish they are.

As we proceed on our miserable way, the roads are thick with mud, like an unappetizing kettle of brown soup with unidentifiable lumps. Other refugees crowd the ravaged streets as well, praying to find their homes intact. Despite the wetness, the pungent odor of smoke still permeates the air. Huge trees are downed; the storm plucked them from the earth by their deep roots. Massive limbs and branches lie scattered everywhere.

Poor Thomas must stop every few feet to clear the debris blocking our path. The same well-loved doll that I mourned during our escape still lies in the same spot. Now, though, a thick layer of sludge covers most of her adorable body, making her almost unrecognizable.

Examples of the storm's far-reaching ruin are everywhere with shattered windows, missing chimneys, and buildings flattened into pathetic heaps. Heavy timber and massive pieces of brick and stone litter the area, sprinkled about like discarded toys. I am aghast at this surreal scenario. My head sweeps back and forth, unable to absorb the immense damage.

Within an instant, an unruly crowd gathers around our dilapidated wagon. Cheers ring out from some kind refugees in front as they shout, "Welcome back, Queen Dolley!"

I wave back, noting the defeat clouding their haggard faces. I shudder despite the soaring heat.

"Aren't you worried about coming back to town?" they call out in trembling voices. Then there is a low murmur, "What if they set their sailors loose on us?"

I stare straight ahead, pretending not to hear their questions. After all, I have the same ones and don't have any answers. Only the evil Cockburn knows. We are at his disposal, and he is without mercy. Of course, our militiamen betrayed us days ago, abandoning the capital city when we needed them most.

As we approach Anna's house, other disheveled residents subject me to their furious stares, frowns and outright glares. Fresh trauma is imprinted upon their souls. I pity them for their suffering; I pity us all. But the worst is their obvious fear. They are too beaten down to hide it.

Soon, though, I encounter an onslaught of outright jeers and hisses. "Look what your worthless little husband did to us!" Their comments are filled with hate, but I don't blame them. They have every right to their monstrous pain. We have all lost so much.

"How's our Queen Dolley now?" they cry out, their voices filled with bitterness. "Why, you've lost your fancy turban! The mighty have fallen, indeed!" Oh, they enjoy scoffing at me and delight in mocking my scruffy outfit.

As we drop off Anna and the children at home, I refuse to get out of the wagon. Instead, I instruct the gardener to take me right to the President's House still in my dowdy dress. I must face it soon enough, so I may as well do it now rather than dread it any longer.

Deep down, though, I pray the damage is not as severe as we believe. I'd give anything in the world to return to our idyllic life right away. If only French John would whisk open the front door and give me his over-the-top flourish.

As we pull around the corner onto Pennsylvania Avenue, heavy smoke descends on us like swollen rain clouds. Overcome with coughing, I exit the wagon and send Thomas to fetch Paul at French John's house. I am anxious to make sure he is all right and find out what transpired during the occupation.

So, there I stand, alone on the edge of President's Park

with my stained kerchief pressed to my nose. Choking and sputtering, I survey the charred ruins of my former home across the street. I'm grateful for the covering as a slew of hot tears pour down my cheeks. Even I cannot keep a brave face right now.

Our once-lovely oasis is now in ruins, a mere skeleton of itself. The roof no longer exists; it is gone. It crashed down along with the floors, ceilings and walls in one huge mass. Only the outer walls survived the blaze, but they are defaced beyond description. The white stone is now scarred, a blackened shell. The cold deluge of rain after the intense heat of the fire cracked them as well.

I am beyond crushed. For once in my life, I am speechless. I can't muster the words to smooth over this atrocity in my mind or anyone else's. Transfixed by my horror, though, I can't tear my eyes away. How is it possible that these smoking ruins were once my beloved sanctuary? I can't comprehend it. Our former home now opens up to the sky.

I put my heart and soul into making our nation proud of the President's House. But alas, the bloody Brits transformed it into a raging inferno, fueled by sheer spite. Now my richly furnished drawing rooms are nothing but smoldering ashes. They are gutted, gone.

I can't come to grips with my losses, but perhaps it's better that way. There are far too many. For some reason, I can only focus on my tiny niece's loss. Ashes are all that remain of her beloved dollhouse. I understand how disappointed my little namesake will be. After all, we both lost our identical homes.

To my great dismay, the catty wife of a Federalist Congressman sidles over to me. I brace myself for her thinly veiled insults. Living up to my low opinion of her, she launches right in with a simpering smile.

"What a pity they caught your husband so unprepared.

Why, he even lost your home," she muses in a breezy manner as if discussing a garden party. "I heard the smoke was visible all the way to Baltimore. That's forty-five miles away. How embarrassing."

"Indeed, it is quite a shame," I mutter.

"You know Cockburn took one of your fancy red cushions with him, don't you?" she blabs, raising her eyebrows.

Aghast, I twist my head and stare at her for a moment. "What did you say?"

"He wanted to remind himself of your...well...your seat."

A wave of righteous anger sweeps over me as the bitter taste of bile rises in my throat.

With no heed for my feelings, she persists. With a light-hearted giggle, she reports that he also stole Jemmy's commander in chief hat as well as his messages to me from the battlefield. Why does this shrew of a woman insist on torturing me with her cruel gloating?

We are supposed to be on the same side, rooting for America to persevere through this colossal crisis. Alas, that isn't the case. She's long forgotten that I was the first person to call on her when she arrived in Washington City and that I spent months introducing her around town. Tempted to utter something I would enjoy but later regret, I stalk away from her.

Throngs of refugees study me with narrowed eyes, gawking at my pathetic dress and trying to discern whether the catastrophe has broken my spirit. Needless to say, I wonder the same.

I whirl around to face the bewildered crowd gathered behind me, declaring, "We shall rebuild Washington City. The enemy shall not frighten a free people." Thankfully, my anger fuels me to speak with a boldness that my wounded soul doesn't feel.

Cheers of "Huzzah!" ring out which bring the first genuine smile to my lips since I can't recall. I may not have a home anymore, but I am at home. Washington City is our nation's home, and I will do everything in my power to keep it so.

CHAPTER 25
DESTRUCTION AND DESPAIR
AUGUST 28, 1814

Retreating from the crowd, I wander back to Anna's in a daze, trying to recall when I was last alone during daylight hours. A dejected Paul sits on the front steps waiting for me, his face stained with tears. He's hunched over his violin, playing a melancholy song. I'm heartened that he was able to save his most precious belonging after we fled.

"Paul, my dear boy, how did you fare? Are you well?" I can't imagine his trauma.

"I'm fine, just fine, Miss Dolley." He nods a few times, but avoids looking at me. "French John took good care of me."

"Well, I'm so glad to hear it. There's been danger lurking everywhere."

"Yes, ma'am. It was plenty scary around here."

"What did you see?" I plunk down next to him without even bothering to wipe away the layer of ashes. This ratty dress is already so filthy that I don't care.

He gives me a sidelong glance but says nothing.

"It's all right, Paul. You can tell me the truth, no matter how ugly it is. I want to know what really happened."

"You sure, Miss Dolley?" He tilts his head and finally looks me in the eye.

I purse my lips together and nod.

"Well, right away, people were walking right into the President's House and grabbing things." The words spill out of his small frame in a rush.

"Really?" I growl. "Those Brits are such scoundrels."

"No, ma'am, it was our people, people from Washington City." He lowers his head.

"*Americans* were doing this?" I'm flabbergasted.

"Yes'm, lots of them." He bobs his head. "The Brits weren't even here yet. They took anything they could lay their hands on. Lamps, mirrors, plenty of dresses and shawls, and some men took them pretty new sofas right out the front door. Then they came back for the big ole grandfather clock."

"They even took our grandfather clock?" My stomach clenches. "That's sickening."

"Yes, Miss Dolley. They were like vultures." He hangs his head. "I wanted to stop them, but I didn't know how." He rubs the back of his hand across his moist eyes.

"It's not your fault, Paul, not at all." I pat him on the shoulder. "But I'm disgusted. For years I invited those people into our home as treasured guests, and then they robbed us at our weakest moment. What a sad insight to human nature!"

Paul stands up and stares at the ground. "Well, after the citizens cleared out, Cockburn rode up on a white horse wearing a fancy gold hat, and then he went inside with his soldiers. I was peeking in the windows, but they didn't pay me any mind." He stops, looking sheepish.

"I'm horrified those brutes entered the President's House."

He hesitates, but I wave my hand, urging him to continue. "The soldiers sat down right away and ate your meal for Mr. Madison. Of course, they drank all the wine, too. They even toasted to the King and the Prince Regent. One of them found Mr. Madison's hat and raised it on his bayonet. Then they all yelled, 'Down with Madison.'" He looks down, his cheeks scarlet.

"Paul, you are not to blame." I pat his arm. "Keep going."

"But Cockburn, he didn't eat anything. He kept walking all around, looking at everything he could find. Then he went upstairs all by himself for a long time. Finally, he came back down carrying Mr. Madison's medicine cabinet with a big stack of his ledgers on top."

"Outrageous," I cry, jumping to my feet and putting my hands on my hips. "Why would that cad take something so personal?" Paul looks over at me, his puffy eyes filled with concern. "Don't worry about the ledgers," I reassure him. "I got the important papers out. The coarseness is what bothers me."

Paul kicks at the muddy ground. "They all went outside and smashed the windows. Then they lit the torches and threw them inside the broken glass at the same time. The fire took over the house really fast, ruining everything. Their uniforms were all red, so they looked like they were on fire, too."

"If only that was true," I exclaim. "All my work with Mr. Latrobe, all those renovations, gone in an instant! It just breaks my heart." It's all I can do not to break down in sobs right in front of the poor boy.

"The fire lit up your drawing rooms so bright, ma'am." He looks up at me, his teary eyes round like moons. "I could've read a whole book outside without a candle."

"Goodness gracious! That is the work of the devil." I shudder. "Did they finally leave then?"

"Everybody but Cockburn. He went across the way to Mrs. Suter's boarding house, and I followed behind him. Miss

Dolley, that poor lady was so scared, I thought she was going to faint right there."

"Oh, no, that sweet woman!" I moan.

"Cockburn smiled at her, real mean, and says, 'Madam, I've come to sup with you.'" Paul stops and takes in a huge breath. "Then he made her blow out all the candles. He wanted to eat his dinner by the light of the fire at the President's House."

"The swine!"

Paul opens his mouth to continue, but I cut him off. "Thank you, Paul, but that's enough. I can't bear another word right now."

He nods, hanging his head again as tears trickle down his cheeks.

Thankfully the ever-kind Margaret visits me at Anna's cozy place during the children's nap that afternoon. I am so proud of them, such brave little nomads coping so well during such a terrible time. For a few minutes, she and I do our best, pretending the evil Cockburn didn't upend our lives. But he did, and our best is not good enough.

For once neither children nor strangers lurk in the background, tracking my every movement. At long last, I can let my guard down with a true friend. We fall into a bear hug, sharing tears of anguish at the wretched state of our country. Such destruction and confusion I've never experienced, not even during the Revolution. I'm so overcome by depression and crippling despair that I can't even speak through my weeping. How my whole heart mourns for America. Oh, we set such a gloomy scene.

Soon our immeasurable sadness morphs into unbridled fury. "How I wish I put a cannon in every window, set them all ablaze and never left," I fume, balling my hands into fists. "If only we had ten thousand men to sink our enemy into a bottomless pit." I release my hands, letting them drop onto the settee. "But of course, we don't. All we can do is pray those scoundrels won't pay us a second visit—or wreak havoc on Baltimore next."

Then almost in a panic, I pour out my mountain of troubles on her, altogether too many to count. "Where will Jemmy and I live? We can't stay with Anna more than a few days. It's unseemly for the president of the United States to be without a suitable home. And how can our Federal Government return to Washington City and actually conduct its business here? After all, where could Congress meet this fall? I doubt we have a room large enough to fit them all, not anymore."

"Of course, the Treasury is gone as well as the State Department, but at least someone saved our meager cash reserve." Margaret looks down at her lap and shakes her head.

"I hope Mr. Pleasanton over at State ignored that idiot Armstrong and sent our Founding Documents to safety like Jemmy directed him." I release a gloomy sigh. "I can't imagine losing them forever. It's too hideous to contemplate."

"We must pray for that," she agrees, raising her head. "But there is one piece of good news to share with you, Dolley. The Brits spared the Patent Office, thank God. Dr. Thornton convinced them that destroying those inventions would hurt the entire world, not just America."

I let out a huge exhale.

Of course, sweet Margaret bears the weight of many heartbreaking woes herself. "That beast also destroyed our office, the only private building in his sights." Her face crumples. "It just breaks my heart!"

"Heavens, no!" I clap a hand to my chest.

"Yes, indeed. Of course, he had to avenge us for calling him the Ruffian," she growls, rolling her eyes.

"There's never been a more accurate nickname." I make a gagging noise.

"At first, he intended to burn it down. Thanks be to God, the ladies who live next door pleaded with him. They were afraid the flames would leap to their homes."

"And they most certainly would've!"

"So, he returned at dawn and ordered his henchmen to throw every single printing press into the street. First he made sure they destroyed every 'C' so we can't write anything about him."

"I expect no less from that egotist," I reply, rolling my eyes.

Finally, Jemmy's familiar figure enters Anna's doorway, and I fly into his arms. With unbridled enthusiasm, I nearly knock him backward into Secretary of State Monroe, but I still refuse to let go. Of course, the poor soul is shattered. He looks so distraught, not to mention exhausted after riding nonstop for five days in his fragile health. After all, he is now in his mid-sixties and nearly died a year ago.

"I can't imagine anything more heinous," he laments once we are finally alone. "Our feeble militia ran away without putting up a fight, and then the enemy burned our capital city and our home." His tone turns scathing. "I certainly hope they choked on our victory dinner left on the table."

Hanging my head, I don't dare tell him they toasted to King George and his son, the Prince Regent, with our crystal wine goblets.

"I insisted on riding by the President's House on our way here." Tears stream down Jemmy's face. "It's the most magnificent and melancholy ruin I ever beheld." He pauses to mop his eyes with his handkerchief. "The only saving grace is knowing the wind must've snapped the Union Jack right off the flagpole at the Capitol. At least we didn't suffer the indignity of it flying over the city for long."

Jemmy frowns. "Of course, I'm even more grateful that Tom's son-in-law was able to unseat Randolph in the last election after seven terms. I couldn't suffer through his gloating. After all, this is exactly what he predicted. But I can't dwell on that now or I'll go mad."

"Did you see the headline in the *London Courier?*" he asks, changing the subject.

I shake my head, dreading his response.

"War America Would Have, And War She Has Got." He releases an agonized sigh. "It's true, though. What a catastrophe, and it's all my fault. They are right. After all, I'm the president of the United States and its commander in chief. This is my life sentence—I will have to live with this every day until I draw my last breath."

All I can do is tuck his head on my shoulder and hold his hand. We sob for our country and ourselves, both wounded on so many levels. I can't help but wonder if we will ever recover from this abomination.

I've never experienced such heartache, not even when my first husband John Todd and our baby William died. Of course, grief wracked the core of my soul, but I didn't feel responsible for their deaths. They were just two of the 5,000 victims who succumbed to yellow fever. Now, though, guilt plagues Jemmy and me both. We could've done more, listened more, negotiated more, or overruled the incompetent Armstrong much earlier to prevent this epic tragedy.

Shame on us, and what great shame it is. I cannot bear the weight of it, but we must move forward for the sake of our damaged country. We owe it to our countrymen to improve this horrific situation. Worse than any nightmare, this is real.

"I don't know where we shall live after here," Jemmy mutters in a forlorn voice. "But we can't leave Washington City. We can't let them win. Plus, if we move the capital city up north, the South will lose its power. But I do need to find somewhere to work soon."

"Absolutely. We must stay." I nod, staring down at my

knotted hands. "Thank goodness for Anna and her family. They're so kind to let us steal any sense of tranquility they have left." I leave the rest unsaid; it's too dismal. Otherwise the president of the United States and his wife would be without a home, crushing the American spirit even more. I pray we can find something suitable since housing is so limited, even before this despicable invasion.

By the next day, Margaret and her husband accomplish an astounding feat. The *National Intelligencer* is back in full operation once again, even releasing a brand-new issue. Of course, they also restored every 'C' to working order and used it to malign vile Cockburn all the more. I pray their fortitude will hearten their demoralized readers.

Full of its usual vigor, the paper calls me the "bravest soldier" under the bold headline, 'The Spirit of the Nation Is Roused!' Word spreads like the fires that decimated our public buildings. The next day they run a poem in my honor, entitled "Mistress Dolley! Long live she!" I am taken aback. It is quite rare for the press to address a woman in such a direct manner. Unfortunately, their stinging criticism of Jemmy's leadership destroys any warm feelings.

Through it all, though, my heart nearly bursts with pride for the Great Little Madison. The mound of insults heaped on him don't deter him in the least from performing his executive duties. Of course, they cause him great distress, but they don't break his spirit.

Refusing to stay behind closed doors for even a moment, he conducts a full tour of inspection with his trusty Secretary of State Monroe, facing the epic trail of wreckage with the dignity of a true commander in chief. He is calm, resolute, and determined to show the world that our government will prevail through this crisis. Through it all, he also remains his kind self, stopping to reassure throngs of dispirited troops and citizens. I couldn't love him more.

Unfortunately, the damage to the Navy Yard is worse than all the other public buildings combined. Hysterical citizens flock to Jemmy, begging him to surrender Washington City if Cockburn should return with his powerful army.

"Never!" shouts Jemmy without a glimmer of hesitation. "We will defend the city to the very last!"

"No one will approach them," declares the gallant Monroe. "They're all damned rascals from highest to lowest." Then he takes it a step further, threatening to punish any attempt to capitulate with his own bayonet.

In addition, many disgusted militiamen approach Jemmy, refusing to serve another hour with Armstrong as Secretary of War. It's a good thing Armstrong himself wasn't there. They would've torn him limb from limb, but perhaps Jemmy may have enjoyed that.

At long last, Jemmy calls for Armstrong's resignation, replacing him with Monroe who will continue to serve as Secretary of State as well. For the first time in our country's short history, political necessity requires a Secretary to play two roles. Margaret, Anna and I toast to the wonderful news of Armstrong's demise, so long overdue.

Then my brave Jemmy sets off to pay special homage to our besieged Capitol. How I treasure the memories of witnessing countless speeches there that stirred my soul. Alas, America's most famous landmark is now a pile of smoldering ruins and ashes. Apparently, Cockburn gave a sarcastic toast to "Jemmy's health" in our gorgeous Hall of Representatives, and conducted a mock vote amongst his troops whether to set it ablaze. Needless to say, they all yelled "aye" in unison. Bringing this national horror to a crescendo, they piled up our cherished mahogany furniture and lit a soaring bonfire for the ages.

Within minutes, a confidential envelope arrives personally

addressed to Jemmy. I stare at it all day, imagining the ghastly news it must contain.

Upon his return, his face is as white as fresh-picked cotton, and he appears twenty years older. "The skylights in the Hall of Representatives melted away and so did the huge marble Statue of Liberty," he blurts out amidst spells of coughing, even before removing his round black hat.

"The skylights are *gone*?" I'm horrified. "Really? And the statue, too? I can't believe it!"

"But that's not all, not by a long shot. The roof and the soaring dome are both gone, too; they crashed down into the cellar along with the entire chamber. The only thing left is a massive haze of black smoke."

"It's all gone? What about those magnificent columns?"

"They're still standing, but barely. They're broken and cracked, on the verge of collapse. Only a few sad arches remain in the Senate. The elegant draperies and carpets are no more. Such complete destruction I've never seen with my own eyes."

"Thankfully, though, one miracle did take place. The vaulting in the Supreme Court survived the inferno." He puts his palms together and looks upward. "And I did get word that Pleasanton managed to save the Founding Documents. They're way out in Virginia hidden in a barn."

"Oh, thank God for that." Biting my lip, I hand him the suspicious letter.

"What new tragedy befalls us now?" He frowns as he rips it open.

Within an instant, though, his lips turn up in a genuine smile, and he waves the paper in the air.

"What is it?" I'm baffled. Surely, he's lost his mind or perhaps I have. "Did something good happen?" I feel silly uttering such words. Happy news is way beyond the realm of possibilities right now.

"Yes, it actually did as a matter of fact. Jefferson wrote a letter on my behalf to the paper. Listen to this, dearest. 'Had Washington himself been at the head of our affairs, the same event would probably have happened.' Then he commended me on my management. Why, he even called me the greatest man in the world." He lets out a long exhale. "How that bolsters my spirits, even coming from my closest friend."

Alas, his face returns to a frown. "Then again, there's horrible graffiti scrawled all over the ruins of the Capitol in charcoal. 'James Madison is a rascal, a coward, and a fool.' At this point I'm tempted to agree."

"Jemmy, I've never heard anything further from the truth," I scoff.

"I must confess to one bright spot," he stage-whispers, even though we are alone at Anna's. "They erected a mock gallows and hung Armstrong in effigy." He drops his voice even more. "But the best part is the sign, 'Armstrong the Traitor.'"

He hangs his head. "However, the ugly truth is that I'm the biggest fool of all. After all, I hired him and didn't fire him when he betrayed me over and over again."

"But now I must tell you the worst line of all." He stares down at the floor. "Someone wrote, 'George Washington founded this city after a seven-year war with England. James Madison lost it after a two-year war.'" He looks up at me, his eyes tortured. "We are the laughingstock of the world, and I can't escape that horrible wood smoke. Even in my dreams, I can still smell it."

"It's not over yet, Jemmy," I murmur, swallowing the lump in my throat. "I still believe in you and many others do, too."

CHAPTER 26
THE END OF AMERICA?
AUGUST 29, 1814

"**M**y dear Presidentess, I am here at your service," announces French John, marching into Anna's parlor with a wry grin and Polly perched on his shoulder. He opens his arms in a courtly bow, full of his usual charming theatrics. Ah, leave it to him to bring a fleeting surge of joy into my life, counteracting my profound misery.

"Queen Dolley, I love you!" Polly screeches, flapping her way over to me in a blur of bright green feathers.

I tear up as she coos in my ear and nuzzles my neck, but she soon fades into a gloomy mood. Then a few minutes later, fury overcomes her. She launches into a string of French swear words too awful to repeat. I cannot fault her. After all, her shifting moods mirror my own.

"When shall we move you into your lovely new home?" he offers.

"What home? I have none as you know," I snap back, my initial amusement gone in a flash. "No teasing, John, not now."

"I'm serious, Mrs. Madison. Colonel Tahoe just agreed to

rent the Octagon House to you. The French ambassador is packing his bags, so it should be ready soon."

"Oh, John, thank you! That is the most wonderful news I've heard in months." My face feels stretched in an odd way. After some reflection, it dawns on me that I'm actually smiling.

Once the corpse of the President's House finally cools off, French John digs in the ashes overflowing from the cellar. He unearths some iron pots and pans and even excavates the massive kitchen range. To my delight, our oven is still intact. Even more amazing, it remains in working order. What a miracle!

With his usual good cheer, he also presents me with new spoons, molds, and buckets for my iced creams. Lastly, he tells me to close my eyes and hold out my hands. When I oblige, a tiny glass bottle drops into my open palms. As my eyes flicker open, I beam. After all the appalling sights and gut-wrenching losses of the last few days, my eyes are feasting on a new bottle of my favorite lilac perfume. How he managed to obtain is well beyond me, but I am so touched. I douse myself right away which soothes my anxious soul.

❧

THANKFULLY AN INSPIRING TALE OF COURAGE BECOMES THE topic of every conversation in America, encouraging us all just when we need it most:

In September 1814, two sisters from Massachusetts scared off hundreds of invading British sailors. From their family's lighthouse in Scituate Harbor, the teenagers spot an enemy warship and devise a clever ruse. While hidden from view, they play 'Yankee Doodle' on their fife and drum as loud as they can, pretending to lead a mighty militia. When their music drifts over to the rowboats headed to shore, the evil invaders panic and turn back. In their haste to make a swift retreat, a sailor is knocked overboard, and they must stop to retrieve him. The girls become national heroes, dubbed the Lighthouse Army of Two.

Huzzah for these brave and clever girls!

CHAPTER 27
BALTIMORE IS NEXT
SEPTEMBER 1814

Much to our horror, the British troops are back on the march just a few days later. This time, though, they are headed north. Just as we feared all along, Baltimore is their next target.

"But they already torched Washington City," I lament. "Isn't that enough revenge, even for them?"

"No, unfortunately not. This isn't over, not by a long shot." Jemmy rolls up his sleeves. "They obviously insist on punishing us some more. Well, at least that stubborn Armstrong was right about one thing." He rolls his eyes. "The British do intend to attack Baltimore. Of course, that's only after invading Washington City with no opposition thanks to him."

Thankfully the burning of Washington City has also lit a roaring flame of patriotism across the country, even among the Federalists. Right away the gutsy people of Baltimore rally 15,000 amateur soldiers to defend their homeland, including many volunteers who pour in from many other states. With furious intensity, they work around the clock, digging earthworks and constructing elaborate fortifications that surround the city. They are determined to repel the British at all costs.

Only three weeks after the invasion of Washington City, the British attack by land on September 12 at North Point, just outside of Baltimore. Thanks be to God, our sharp-shooters inflict a shocking amount of damage, pushing them back, and even killing their Commanding General Ross. Jemmy sends my cousin Francis Scott Key to negotiate the release of Dr. William Beanes, imprisoned for jailing British troops who stole food from farms near Bladensburg.

However, the British invade again early the next morning, this time by sea. Their thirty ships include heavy frigates and bomb vessels filled with Congreve rockets, long-range mortars, and thousands of shells weighing over two-hundred pounds each. They attack Fort McHenry, the star-shaped brick fortress that guards the entrance to Baltimore Harbor. It is no secret that if the Baltimoreans lose this crucial battle, their city will fall and perhaps our entire country, too.

THAT NIGHT, JEMMY AND I HUDDLE ON A TATTERED SETTEE at the Octagon House and wait for news, just as we did all day long. It's so late I've lost track of time. By now, we must be well into the wee hours of the morning of September 13. Something familiar about the date nags at me, but I can't remember why.

Of course, we moved in here empty-handed, so we're grateful for anywhere to sit. Now I would welcome the shabby furniture that I mocked during my first walk-through of the President's House. At least we'd have the luxury of another place to worry. I don't care much for this house or its exorbitant rent, and I'm convinced its air is bad. Right when we first moved in, Jemmy and several servants fell sick.

However, I remind myself to thank God for the leaky roof over our heads and damp cellar beneath us.

As unnerving bolts of thunder crack in the vicinity, I stare out the parlor window. Ominous darkness covers the lovely view stretching across the farms to the broad Potomac.

The torrential downpour pounds outside with a steady drumbeat. It sounds like British soldiers are marching into Washington City to ravage it once again, but I know that my exhaustion and paranoia are working against me. In reality, they are quite occupied trying to conquer Baltimore.

We stare at the walls, straining our ears for the sound for footsteps. I have to say something, anything, to break the oppressive silence hovering over us like a ton of granite. Otherwise I shall go mad. "What a terrible storm. How our poor friends in Baltimore must be suffering right now. Hopefully God will work in our favor once again, just like He sent that hurricane here to put out those hellish fires."

Bolts of thunder clap overhead as poor Jemmy wrings his hands. Tears pool up in his haggard eyes with gray bags hanging underneath like sandbags. I swear his face has a new layer of wrinkles every time we exchange woebegone glances. "Oh, what destruction I brought upon our poor country," he mutters. "The American people trusted me to lead them, and I've let them down in every way possible." He looks down at the floor. "We can't survive much more."

"Jemmy, we'll make it through this," I encourage him, doing my best to project the confidence that I don't feel. "Let's not underestimate our brothers in arms. The people of Baltimore won't let us down. They're determined to fight to the death."

"But darling, how can you be so sure? Especially after everyone in Washington City fled like Lucifer was chasing them." His voice cracks. "Who can say they won't do the same up there?"

"Jemmy, you and I both experienced the horror of watching Washington City burn. Don't forget the Baltimoreans know it, too! They're only forty miles away; they saw it from their rooftops going up in flames, and they've been preparing for weeks. Even the children are helping to dig trenches. They'll do anything to prevent the Union Jack from flying over Baltimore."

"Yes, you're right." He throws his shoulders back. "They've done a magnificent job establishing defensive lines and an entire chain of forts all around city."

"Remember we only had a few minutes notice here in Washington City, thanks to that pathetic fool Armstrong." I wag my index finger at him and wink. "I told you to fire him a long ago. But the people of Baltimore understand what's at stake—their homes and our very country. Mark my words, the Brits have made a colossal mistake this time. They'll soon regret calling them a nest of pirates!"

"I hope you're right again, my dear." Jemmy cracks a wan smile. "You've always been my most valuable advisor. At Bladensburg, those burning Congreve rockets terrified everyone, including me, with their horrible hissing. Just picture a long stick spinning through the air at you with a canister of gunpowder, tar and shrapnel attached."

"I would've run away, too," I admit.

"But at least now we know the truth—they're completely useless," he declares. "The safest place to stand is where they're supposed to land." He smirks. "And it even rhymes. Oh, the irony of it all. But it's true, though. Serves them right."

"The brave people of Baltimore are raising my sagging spirits. Their defiance encourages me so," I struggle to fight back tears. "But I feel so ashamed. It's my job to raise theirs."

"Don't be so hard on yourself, my dearest. If there's one

thing we've learned from this ghastly war, we're all Americans. By God, we all need each other, especially right now."

"We certainly do." I dab at my eyes as they threaten to spill over. "I'm amazed that I have any tears left."

"Dare I remind you, my dear, three weeks ago there was no braver person in Washington City than you. You were the one Cockburn most wanted to capture, yet you were among the last to leave."

"I just did my duty, the same as you heading out to the battlefield. Of course, I'm worried about Baltimore, but I also fear for Betsy and her son. What a relief that Payne is overseas now, although we've still heard nothing from him."

"No need to worry, my dear," Jemmy treasures me. "Rest assured, the British have no interest in Betsy and Bo anymore. They've already defeated Napoleon, so capturing them now serves no purpose. However, those Redcoats might enjoy feasting their eyes on her." He cracks a fleeting smile. "As for our boy, he'll show up. He always does, even if just to ask us to cover his bills."

I let out a cackle. It's been so long that I'm surprised to remember how. I reach over and caress his haggard face. "You're right, thank you. You're so good to all of us."

Suddenly the significance of September 13 comes to me.

"Jemmy, do you know what day it is?"

"Our day of reckoning?" he responds in a morose voice.

"No, it's our anniversary. We've been married twenty years today."

"Dearest, I'm so sorry." He takes my hand and kisses it. "I can't imagine life without you by my side and never more so than now."

"Well, I forgot, too. We've had quite a few distractions. It's for better or worse."

"Let's pray it won't get any worse."

Out of the corner of my eye, I spot Jemmy's small

tricorne hat next to the front door. He must've put it there in case he needs to make a hasty visit to Congress in the dead of night. Of course, that would mean the worst scenario imaginable, the fall of Baltimore. That possibility sends shivers running down my spine. What will become of our beloved United States?

CHAPTER 28
GLORIOUS NEWS
SEPTEMBER 13, 1814

Once again, we sit in silence awaiting an update. I gaze at Jemmy's trusty lantern, lost in my tumultuous thoughts. It burns at an even pace for a few minutes and then flickers, like my heart vacillating between fragile faith and sheer terror. I doze off, but when a horse whinnies nearby, I awake with a start. Seconds later, someone pounds on the front door, sending an ominous echo throughout the empty Octagon House. I hope Anna and her family don't wake up. They were so kind to come and keep us company here on such a dreadful night.

Clad only in his nightshirt, Jemmy scurries to answer it. I scoot along behind him, delirious with fatigue, not caring that I must look a fright. I can't remember the last time I ran a comb through my hair or even changed the stained apron on my gray housedress. What does that matter when we're on the brink of losing our country? Even the most splendid dress from Paris holds no longer holds any meaning for me. That's just as well since I lost my entire wardrobe, the servants' clothing, and our home with all its furnishings less than a month ago.

A pimply-faced messenger wearing sodden street clothes stands on the steps in the driving rain. He looks off into the darkness, his eyes focused on the bright flashes of lightning. Still avoiding eye contact, he raises a dripping arm to wipe his brow and then stares down at the ground.

Jemmy steps forward and extends his petite hand. Even while stooped, the boy is a full head taller. He still doesn't look up, so Jemmy reaches out and touches his shoulder. "Come now, young man, please come in. Why, thank you for coming all this way. Please do come in." It's uncanny how Jemmy's shyness disappears when he notices that someone else is in pain. His kindness to this awkward lad, even during the worst of circumstances, warms my aching heart.

"Yes, sir," mumbles the boy as he stumbles inside. "Sorry I can't hardly talk. I ain't never met no president before." He takes a quick glance in my direction. "Or the Lady President neither."

"We're just Americans tonight, son." Jemmy forces his pressed lips into a tiny smile. "What's your name?"

"Um." He pauses as if he can't recall. "Um, Sam."

"Welcome, Sam. Please tell, what news do you have for us?"

"Mr. President, the battle, it's still going on." Then he talks faster and faster, spitting it all out in a torrent. His eyes dart around, looking everywhere but at Jemmy. "The Royal Navy keeps sending them mortar bombs roaring at us, shaking the whole fort. I swear there been a thousand so far, at least one a minute. And shooting plenty of them rockets, too, louder than thunder. They lit up the sky, but the rain and fog got so thick nobody could see nothing. But, sir, you'd be right proud of us. None of us got real training, but we're giving them everything we got!"

"Thank you, Sam." Jemmy nods. "You're a fine soldier. I am very proud. I've never been so proud of my country as I

LIBBY CARTY MCNAMEE

am tonight. God bless you, and God bless Baltimore. But I do have one more question for you. Any word on Mr. Francis Scott Key and the prisoner, Dr. Beanes?"

"Well, Mr. Key went onboard with the Royal Navy to see about getting Dr. Beanes released." He hesitates as his chin quivers. "But then, then the battle started. Nobody seen him since."

Jemmy's head drops an inch, and his jaw clenches.

Paul helps Sam dry off as best he can, while I offer refreshments. When Sam balks, I insist. Sukey serves him some coffee with stale bread and jam, which is all we have. He gobbles down every morsel, cramming it all into his mouth. Then he guzzles down the coffee so fast that I fear he will choke. Within seconds, he lets out a resounding belch and blushes all the way to his scalp.

Jumping to his feet, young Sam heads back out into the eerie darkness that swallows him up in seconds. Again the hours crawl by with no word. When Anna and her brood awake and wander in, we tell the children to play in their rooms while the adults stare at the hands on the clock. The vicious storm ends at some point, but we don't even notice.

Finally, come mid-morning, a horse whinnies outside. Within seconds, we welcome the sweet relief of fierce pounding on our door. What a melodious sound. At this point, I'd rather receive horrible news than wait another bloody minute.

Jemmy sprints to the door and whisks it open, still in his dressing gown. If I wasn't so paralyzed by fear and weariness, I would so enjoy teasing him. After all, I've never seen him move with such speed. But I won't delay the news, not even for that.

Much to our surprise, Sam is back on our doorstep again. "Mr. President, I begged to come back so I could be the one to tell you." This time he stands tall in the brilliant sunshine reflecting off the lakes of mud. More importantly, he wears a proud smile as he leans forward to shake Jemmy's hand.

"It's all over!" he shouts, shaking both fists in the air. "When daylight came, there was lots of smoke and haze, but our flag was still there. After twenty-five hours of those red rockets and exploding cannonballs, the Brits finally gave up. At seven this morning, the whole fleet done sailed back downriver. They never got an inch into Baltimore Harbor!"

"Huzzah!" Jemmy shouts, louder than he's ever been.

"Then we fired off our morning gun over Fort McHenry and raised the biggest American flag in the whole world, right there in all the smoke. It's forty-two feet across and thirty feet high. Each stripe is two feet wide. I swear it was the only dry thing left in Baltimore. What a moment of glory. And the band played 'Yankee Doodle.'" He smiles. "Oh, Mr. President, I won't never forget that!"

"Thank you, Sam." Jemmy grabs his hand and pumps it with remarkable vigor for his frail frame. "You've served our country admirably. Please give the people of Baltimore our deepest gratitude. I've never been quite so proud of a nest of pirates!"

"Before I forget, there's one more thing, Mr. President! Mr. Key and Dr. Beanes, they're both safe. The Brits made Mr. Key stay on their ship all night during the battle. But then they let him and Dr. Beanes go right when they pulled out. Mr. Key watched the entire battle from the deck and wrote a brilliant poem about it."

"Thank you, Sam. That's wonderful news. What a tremendous relief, and I look forward to reading the poem."

"They're printing it on broadbills right now. I'll make sure one gets delivered here." Sam gives Jemmy an awkward salute. "Thank you, Mr. President."

"And you, too, Lady President," he says, looking over at me. I reach out and hug the dear boy. "You're even prettier than everyone says," he blurts, his face tomato-red. Before I can offer him some more stale bread and jam, he races down the steps, calling over his shoulder, "My captain made me promise no dilly-dallying."

Standing on the doorstep, Jemmy and I wave goodbye as he gallops away. Right there with our door wide open, we grab each other in a long embrace and sob. At long last, the tears we shed are happy ones.

CHAPTER 29

THE OCTAGON HOUSE

T he Octagon House is an elegant structure facing the corner of New York Avenue and 18th Street. We are so grateful to occupy it, but it isn't nearly as grand as the President's House. However, the close location to the charred ruins and Jemmy's circular study above the entryway are both ideal.

Bursting with euphoria over our miraculous victory in Baltimore, we are even more thrilled when the Brits finally abandon their abusive Chesapeake Campaign once and for all. I vow to entertain as soon as possible in our new temporary home.

"Every stitch of my wardrobe is gone," I confide to Margaret over coffee and generous slices of Woodbury cinnamon cake slathered with fairy butter. "The thought of it pains me, not just because of the clothes; it's the lost memories. But what a wonderful excuse to buy new dresses, even more fashionable this time."

"That's the spirit, Dolley. Here's to even more elaborate turbans!" Margaret jokes as we toast with our cups and indulge ourselves in a second piece of cake with even more fairy butter.

Within a few short weeks, I am ready. My first drawing rooms at the Octagon House take place just two days after Congress returns to this mournful shell of a town to meet at the Patent Office.

Chagrined that my bronze lamps lie in a melted heap just a few blocks away, I brainstorm and soon come up with a creative solution. I direct the servants to hold flaming torches, casting our temporary home in a warm glow. Unfortunately, we also lack the piano, elegant linens, mirrors, paintings, busts, carpets, and any decent furniture, not to mention my custom-painted Grecian chairs.

However, these drawing rooms do have one thing that is the same. They have me. Wearing my new lilac perfume thanks to French John, I dress in my most glamorous gown yet, featuring rich colors and lush fabrics adorned with lace and fine trim. Even without my usual trappings, the record turnout soothes my shattered soul. Perhaps there is reason for hope after all, despite the sour Federalists who boycotted the event.

At least the ruins are no longer smoking. However, my heart is still bruised, and I fear it will remain so forever.

CHAPTER 30
NEW ORLEANS UNDER SIEGE
NOVEMBER 1814 - JANUARY 1815

Dear Paul ferries me around Washington City on my usual rounds. The cool November temperatures are such a treat, as well as the glorious absence of mosquitos feasting on my plump arms. For once, bouncing from rut to rut doesn't bother my joints. At least I have one reason for joy in my soul.

He knows to avoid the public buildings, especially the gutted President's House. It's only two blocks away, but I can't bear the sight of the blackened ruins. They still bring me to tears and always will. Although the roof is gone, the thick sandstone walls still stand. Alas, they are charred and cracked like my heart.

After their initial jeers, the citizens of Washington City come together and forgive me for the most colossal of calamities. Perhaps they realize I am just as miserable as they are. Of course, my fierce protection of General Washington's portrait endeared me to them most of all. I am thankful for my instincts that compelled me to save it from the clutches of the wicked Cockburn. That painting represents America for us all.

Alas, my poor Jemmy remains their scapegoat. Everyone blames him for the heartbreaking destruction and our many national woes. But why him? It isn't fair for so many reasons. When the British first approached, he refused to flee. Instead, he headed straight to the front lines to support the troops, risking his own life. Then after the torching of Washington City, he didn't flinch. Instead, he revived our war efforts right away. Nonetheless, the Federalists will soon gather in Hartford, Connecticut. Those traitors want to secede from our precious union. Jemmy and I fume at their treasonous behavior, but we can't do anything about it.

Negotiations continue in Ghent, Belgium, headed by Treasury Secretary Gallatin. Unfortunately, the reports are quite glum. The British drag out the process as much as possible. Then they make outrageous demands, requiring us to become subservient to them once again. Every day the prospect of peace appears even more distant, discouraging us all the more.

Although Payne remains part of our delegation, vicious rumors swirl that drinking and the nightlife are his main focus rather than his duties. He is still a young man, so I keep faith that he will rise to the occasion, and these wartime hostilities will come to an end. They must. With no other option but crippling despair, I force myself to carry hope in my heart.

Back in mid-September, Major General Andrew Jackson fended off an attack on Mobile, Alabama, while the bulk of the Redcoats were still fighting in Baltimore. Now he seizes Pensacola, Florida, away from the Spanish, preventing the British from landing there. Full of unusual cheer, Jemmy sends news of both victories to Congress.

Now General Jackson warns of a major invasion along the Gulf Coast, and rumors abound. Just in case, Jemmy dispatches a load of ammunition and supplies, but he has no troops to spare. We can only pray the feisty Jackson received bad intelligence. Dear God, please let this loathsome conflict and rampant destruction cease once and for all.

My immediate goal is simple. I must use every resource at my disposal to calm those angry citizens who demand the relocation of our capital to Philadelphia, Cincinnati, or even New York City. Quite frankly, they'd prefer anywhere to avoid the cost of reconstructing Washington City, especially given the dismal state of our finances.

Mark my words. We will *never* agree to move the national seat, especially to the north. General Washington selected these ten square miles himself, and we cannot allow the British to have the satisfaction of chasing us away. In addition, it would only empower those subversive Federalists to criticize Jemmy all the more. They refuse to acknowledge the truth. Jemmy inherited this fine mess from Mr. Jefferson and tried to reason with the nasty British for years. He only declared war as a last resort.

Much to our dismay, Congress will take a vote soon. Hannah, Margaret and I gather for several strategy sessions. Then I schedule an emergency Dove Party. Of course, the focus will be on rebuilding of our national capital here in Washington City.

Paul drives me around town to call on the wives of Jemmy's political adversaries. I hope to transform these ladies into friendly foes and soon genuine friends. Of course, I don't find everyone at home. Along with my calling card, I leave an invitation. In addition to coffee, I plan to serve my usual bouillon and sardine tea toasts, followed by my beloved Williamsburg pound cake. A party is not a party without cake.

Soon the House of Representatives meets in the Patent Office and strikes down the proposal to relocate our capital city. Amazingly enough, the winning margin is even stronger than the original vote to declare war. Huzzah! Jemmy and I savor the sweetness of our hard-fought victory.

Dashing our emboldened spirits, Congress doesn't appropriate any money to start the actual rebuilding. This is an expensive process that will take years. With this setback, now it will take even longer. Suddenly, our achievement feels hollow, and I'm devastated.

As Rosalie and I exit the building and board our carriages, she is surprisingly positive. "The burning of the public buildings is the best thing that's happened in a long time for Washington City. It finally settles the question whether the seat of our government will stay here. In the future they will no longer keep trying to change it."

"Why, Rosalie." I look over and beam at her. "What an excellent point. You've boosted my spirits." These are words I never thought I would utter. The world has truly turned upside down.

When my carriage pulls up in front of the Octagon, I do my best to brush aside my pangs for the President's House. How I miss our life there. I decorated it with such love and made it my true home, as well as America's. Thankfully the pile of calling cards that accumulated during my absence distract me. I scan through the familiar names, a wonderful mix of fellow Republicans and misguided Federalists. I smile, spotting Lucretia Clay, Elizabeth Monroe, and Floride Calhoun at the top of the stack.

Feeling chipper, I trot up the majestic winding staircase as fast as my sad knee will allow. I expect to find Jemmy poring over his treatises and bottomless pile of correspondence, as usual. It seems like he has hardly left his desk since the war began two years ago.

I dart into his study with a huge smile, hoping to distract him.

He sits upright in his chair and gapes at me, ashen-faced.

My stomach plummets, and I stare back. Something dreadful has happened.

"Jemmy, what's wrong?" I spit out.

"Vice President Gerry died a few hours ago." He pauses. "But we have even worse news."

I sink into a nearby chair, grateful to find it before my legs give out.

He holds my gaze for another agonizing moment. Then he picks up a letter and reads in a flat voice, "A British fleet of more than fifty ships has sailed into the Gulf of Mexico."

"No!" I gasp like a feisty mule just kicked me in the belly, and my jaw hangs open.

"Looks like they're headed for New Orleans." He looks over at me, his eyes wide and pupils huge. "If they take it, they'll gain control of the Mississippi River and split the country in two. Then they'll plunder all the goods that have piled up in the warehouses during the blockade. Just the cotton alone is worth fifteen million dollars, the entire price of the Louisiana Purchase."

"Oh, dear God!" I slap a hand to my chest.

"Jackson was right." He hangs his head. "I should've listened to him. At the very least, I should've sent some troops down there to help." His voice gets softer, almost to a whisper. "But the worst part is this letter is already two weeks old."

"Good heavens, what in the world has happened down there since then?" I bring my palms to my cheeks and squeeze my eyes shut.

"I'm terrified to find out, to be honest with you. Our destiny now depends on Louisiana, our newest state, yet I've never set foot in the place or been anywhere near it. Why should the people there feel any allegiance to America?"

"Jemmy, that's not your fault. Louisiana only became a

state two years ago. It's over a thousand miles away, and they barely have any roads, and none of them are decent. Plus, there's a huge wilderness with hostile Indians surrounding it. Even the sea is full of pirates. And they speak French! They're hardly Americans at all."

"Thank God that General Jackson is—or was—already on his way, marching down from Tennessee with his Seventh District troops." Jemmy shakes his head. "I'm glad he's on our side, because I'd hate to fight against him. The Indians nicknamed him Sharp Knife for good reason. Now his troops call him Old Hickory because he's just as tough as the wood and marches right alongside them." He releases a long pent-up sigh. "If anyone can pull this off, it's him, but it seems impossible."

"Jackson may be fierce, but he isn't a miracle worker," I declare, throwing up my hands. I want to say more, but there are no words to describe my anguish.

"Let's hope he is because that's what we need right now." He jumps to his feet and paces back and forth. "Otherwise we're doomed, and they'll steal the entire Louisiana Purchase from us. We only have a handful of Army regulars down there, two small regiments. The Brits have their toughest troops, the same ones who brought down Napoleon and..." He clears his throat and continues, "burned Washington."

"How could I forget?" My hopes are dashed, and I let out an unattractive moan. "Maybe our return to the British kings is inevitable, and we'll be bowing to their Prince Regent soon."

"I can't stand the thought of the Union Jack flying over New Orleans or anywhere else in America for that matter." Jemmy's eyes fill with tears, and I regret my harsh words. I stand behind him, wrapping my arms around his neck as he sits down and reads the letter aloud to me several more times.

Everyone in America must wait for news, testing our

patience and sanity, especially mine. Soon I avoid leaving the house for fear of missing an update. I don't even risk a quick visit to Anna and her children just a few blocks away. Instead, I spend my time peeking out behind the drapes, praying that a messenger will arrive on our doorstep any second.

It's just as well that I don't venture anywhere since a dangerous epidemic called putrid sore throat strikes the area. Of course, this puts an additional damper on Christmas festivities, as if we needed another reason for gloom. Even the delicious smell of soft gingerbread from Mr. Jefferson's recipe wafting through the air doesn't lighten my mood.

At long last, on a frosty morning after the bleak start of 1815, a filthy man hovers outside the parlor window, dressed head to toe in buckskin. An undernourished mare stands alongside him, caked in mud and panting. His warm breath blows billowing clouds into the frigid air. The man takes halting steps toward the house, using his hunting rifle like a cane. His legs are so bowed that he all but staggers.

Slamming down my coffee cup onto its saucer, I hurry out to greet him, not even bothering with my winter coat.

"I brung a letter from Old Hickory, one of the finest men ever to walk this Earth," he hollers, waving a piece of paper over his head. Then he breaks into a huge smile, revealing a mouthful of broken yellow teeth. "I never seen such a loverly lookin' woman in my whole life!" he blurts out and follows with an ear-piercing whistle.

"Welcome to Washington City," I call to him, scurrying down the steps. "I'm Dolley, and we are so grateful to you for making such a difficult trip!"

"Hal Hawkins from Pulaski, Tennessee." He pumps my hand, shaking my arm all the way up to my shoulder, and then touches his bushy beard still laced with frost. "Dolley, did you say?" He blushes, pulls off his coonskin cap and places it over his heart. "Am I really seein' the Lady President? You just as purdy as all the folks say."

I smile, pretending to understand him, but I can barely decipher his twang. "Yes, but please call me Dolley. Please come right inside and rest." I resist the urge to snatch the message out of his dirty hands until I help him up the steps. How I want to turn my nose aside to avoid the noxious stench, but my manners prevent me from doing so.

As we enter the house, he props his hunting rifle by the door, topping it his coonskin cap on top, and hands me the battered envelope. Then he sprawls out on my new velvet settee and unlaces his cracked boots, scattering hunks of dirt across the gleaming floor that Sukey just finished mopping. "What day is it now? I lost count the last time those Injuns were chasin' after me. Nearly caught me then. Never prayed so hard."

"It's Thursday," I reply, bolting up the winding staircase to deliver the letter to Jemmy. "Sukey, please prepare a meal for our guest, Mr. Hawkins," I shout over my shoulder.

"That would be real nice, Miz Dolley," he calls up to me. "I ain't had nothin' but a few squirrels and some moonshine this whole ride. I heard tales about your fancy parties and icey cream."

I race into Jemmy's study, disturbing him reading a thick treatise, and thrust the letter into his hands. As he rips it open, a roach falls onto his desk and crawls toward him. He growls, presses his lips together, and flattens it with his fist. Without bothering to sweep it into the bin, he hunches down in his chair and reads in silence.

"God, help us," he declares, still staring at the letter.

Then he lowers it, shakes his head, and locks eyes with me. "Jackson says there was a disastrous naval battle at Lake Borgne on December 14. The Brits captured all of our gunboats and set off a panic in New Orleans."

I grimace. This does not bode well for our newest state.

"So then Jackson declared martial law, collected everyone's hunting rifles, and drafted all able-bodied men into service, calling them the Sons of Freedom." His voice is flat.

"Martial law! What in the world?" he shouts suddenly, startling me. He drops the letter onto the desk and pounds the flailing roach again. "Taking away people's rights to save freedom? He doesn't have the legal authority! What about the Constitution that I worked so doggedly to create? No emergency justifies taking this type of action!"

I'm aghast. In our many years of marriage, he's never once shouted at anyone, not even a servant.

"But if that's what it takes to save America, I don't care," he mutters with his next breath. "The Constitution won't matter if we don't have a country anymore. There's no time to send troops down there, and we don't have any to send." He shakes his head. "He claims he's going to rally the Creoles, Cajuns, Native Americans, Kentucky woodsmen, slaves, free blacks, profiteers, and even the pirates. Then he wants to blend them with the backwoods militias and volunteers. Good God. Does he really think he can get this makeshift army of barbarians to come together and fight for us?"

"America's fate is in the hands of an unsavory lot of ruffians," I declare as my heart sinks. "There's nothing we can do but pray."

"Now the Brits have the perfect landing zone for their troops." Jemmy grits his teeth. "I bet they've already taken New Orleans, and we just haven't gotten word yet."

He picks up the letter and reads it over again. "Just in case the situation isn't dismal enough, Jackson's got a horrible case of dysentery. He has trouble standing up and can only get down a bowl of rice a day. Dear Lord, what a disaster in the making."

Try as I might, I have no words of comfort to offer. With

tears streaming down my face, I can't hide my overwhelming despair. News of the dire situation in the Gulf of Mexico spreads like the yellow fever that claimed my first husband and sweet baby boy in Philadelphia. Hysteria takes hold, spreading everywhere. The treasonous Federalists call for Jemmy's impeachment, and the House of Representatives considers abandoning Washington City for good.

Our circumstances could not be more dismal. Once again, I conduct a social campaign to support my husband, calling on the frosty Federalist wives multiple times, ignoring their rebuffs. Eventually I wear them down, and they sip coffee and eat spice cake with me at the Octagon House as I inquire about their children and relatives back home.

Day in and day out, we wait, worry and wonder for weeks on end. It's agonizing, but we have no choice. It will take at least two weeks for another message to reach us. Every day we dare to believe we will receive news, but our hopes are dashed over and over.

The divisive Federalists lash out yet again, this time accusing Jemmy of covering up a humiliating defeat down in New Orleans. This absurd accusation shows their blatant disregard for the common good of our nation, igniting a relentless fury in me.

With no update for an eternity, our lives come to a standstill. Overactive nerves paralyze us all. We cannot afford to lose control of New Orleans and the mouth of the mighty Mississippi River. America's longest river is the gateway to the vast western lands of the Louisiana Purchase. Although it is still new territory, its strategic location has already become both our lifeline and our future.

I find it impossible to muster good cheer although everyone relies on me to provide it. Every day Jemmy and I have the same conversation, as if from a script. I start off by complaining, "I thought suffering through the night waiting for news from Baltimore was awful. Little did I know how much more excruciating it would get."

"I've never felt so powerless in my life," he replies. "It's been a month, and a hodgepodge of brand-new citizens out in the wilds of America are deciding our future."

All we can do is hold each other and pray that God grants us a miracle. Nothing less than that can save America now. Jemmy declares a day of public fasting and prayer for the safety and welfare of our country as well as the speedy restoration of peace. I forgo my usual array of treats, get down on my aching knees, and pray with my whole heart.

Just as we reach our breaking point, the cruel forces of nature stretch us even further. A ferocious blizzard strikes Washington City in late January, burying us in several feet of snow. Then the coldest snap in memory sets in. Our only fleeting pleasure is eating flavored snow which makes us shiver all the more.

As if our burdens were not enough, any hopes of receiving news anytime soon are dashed. Road are blocked, bridges closed, and mail delivery becomes an impossible feat. Perhaps we are doomed to stay in this state of limbo forever. I can't help but wonder if this is the end of the American experiment once and for all.

"At the start of the war, Randolph predicted that nature would prove to be our greatest enemy." Jemmy rolls his eyes, bemoaning the massive storm. "He was absolutely right. And you know how much it pains me to admit it."

I can only nod. I do know because it pains me just as much.

Thankfully a bright spot emerges as this dreadful month finally comes to a close. Our dear friend Mr. Jefferson provides us with more support, declaring, "Even if General Washington himself was at the head, the same events probably would've happened."

In addition, he offers the contents of his own vast library to rebuild our torched Library of Congress. This bolsters Jemmy, knowing that Mr. Jefferson loves his books more than people, much like himself. Congress purchases 6,000 volumes, doubling the original collection and broadening its scope.

CHAPTER 31

THE DIRTY SHIRTS PREVAIL

FEBRUARY 1815

By February, we lose any hope of ever receiving news. At this point neither Jemmy nor I care if it's good or bad. We just want to know something, anything.

I direct Sukey and the servants to conduct a full house cleaning and then pitch in myself. At this point, I'm willing to do anything to distract myself from my mountain of worries. I mop each step on the winding staircase by hand. Since my wardrobe is still so limited while I await new fabric, I can't risk dirtying a presentable gown. So, I don the drab farm-house dress from that horrible August day when I returned back to Washington City to confront the destruction.

Dripping with sweat, I work my way up from the bottom while Sukey polishes the front windows. "Miss Dolley, some soldiers are here marching up the front steps," she shrieks out of the blue.

Letting out a whoop, I forget the stairs are still wet and race down. I slip, but thankfully I manage to grab the railing before toppling down the entire flight. Undeterred, I run to the door and throw it open, forgetting all about my tattered housedress.

Two soldiers stare at me, but I'm out of breath. The first is a tall chiseled Marine in a gray military coat with matching red cuffs and collar. He stands at rigid attention, his shiny black hat standing atop his blond head like a cylinder. Without a word, he snaps a stiff salute which I wave off as I wipe my brow with the back of my soapy hand.

"*Bonjou, La Reine Dolley! Ca va?*" says the other soldier with an eager smile. He is smaller with dark hair and eyes, and wears a different uniform.

I can't understand a word. However, I do recognize his distinct Cajun dialect and match his smile. I am relieved that Jemmy speaks French, one of his six languages.

"Private Pierre LeBlanc from Breaux Bridge, Louisiane," chatters the Cajun soldier with his thick accent. "I'm in de militia; ma mere not so happy. My derriere sure is sore after ridin' for long days. But dis news is big, big. *Laissez les bons temps rouler*. Dis is our lucky day!"

Try as I might, I still can't make out a lick, so I just smile and nod. "Please let me take you to Mr. Madison right away. He will be thrilled to see you." I turn on my heel and gesture toward the stairs.

"*C'est bon! Allons!*" The Cajun beams and raises his arm.

Once again, I pretend to understand.

They both take a step forward, so I whisk them up to Jemmy's study. By now, I've totally forgotten about the wet stairs. Thankfully their mud-caked boots are used to much more treacherous terrain. The dirt breaks off in messy chunks and bounces down step-by-step, but I don't care.

With his cylindrical hat, the lanky Marine towers over Jemmy by a foot. He snaps another salute, and Jemmy stands on his tiptoes to return it.

"Mr. President, Lieutenant Ambrose Clark reports on behalf of the United States Marines." The Marine's voice booms with the force of a cannon. "I apologize for my gray jacket which is unauthorized. They ran out of blue cloth a while back. I also regret our delay. Heavy rains and flooding slowed us down."

"Dem bayous all flooded, and dem gators after us everywhere," Private LeBlanc chimes in. "We's just happy to be living. Now we are brudders, us."

"Lieutenant, please don't give it another thought." Jemmy nods. "You both look quite impressive after such an arduous journey. America and I both thank you for your heroic efforts to get here."

"It's been an honor, Mr. President." The Marine hesitates. "Sir, did a messenger from New Orleans arrive here back in December?"

"Yes, Mr. Hawkins from Pulaski, Tennessee. A fine young man."

"Well, sir, Hawkins never made it back to New Orleans." The Marine looks down at the floor. "So General Jackson sent two of us this time."

"Oh dear, I hope he is holed up somewhere safe." Jemmy peers at him. "Son, you look quite familiar. By any chance, are you related to the Clarks of Clark's Mountain in Orange County, Virginia?"

"Yes, sir, that's my family." His eyes shine.

"What a great coincidence. We come from the same small town and meet each other here. Why don't you boys go get yourself a meal down in the cellar while Dolley and I read over this letter? You must be ravenous."

"Ah, ya," smiles the Cajun as they head out the door. "I've got an envie for some gumbo. Did good, us."

Jemmy sits on the edge of his chair, reading every line of the letter with his usual dogged attention to detail.

I want to pepper him with questions, but I hold my breath and force myself to wait.

At long last, his face lights up, warming my heart. How I've missed his winsome smile since this dreadful war began.

With a sudden burst of energy, he springs to his feet and waves the paper in the air, more agile than he's been in years. "By God, he did it! Jackson won the Battle of New Orleans. Old Hickory saved America! His army of total misfits accomplished what our militia in Washington City couldn't."

"Huzzah!" I hop up as well and clap my hands.

He glances down at the letter again and then looks back at me with wide eyes. "The battle was way back on January 8th."

"Oh, my goodness! That was almost an entire month ago!" I'm incredulous.

"Queen Dolley, this Jackson is a hero for the ages!" He throws his hands in the air. "His army achieved immortal glory, a true miracle in New Orleans!" He beams. Joy radiates from his haggard face.

"Well, aren't you full of chatter all of a sudden?" I tease him.

He bends over, roaring. I've never seen him so rowdy, but I'm too impatient to enjoy the moment. "Enough theatrics, Jemmy! Read it to me, read it! I want to hear every word!"

"Of course, my dear." He gives me a quick kiss and launches in, his low voice filled with awe as I drink in every incredible word.

JANUARY 9, 1815

Dear President Madison:

As of yesterday, Louisiana is now clear of our enemy. I write to you with great pride from New Orleans at the mouth of the mighty Mississippi, which I can assure you is still part of the United States, now and forevermore. Trust me, we have crippled the British, and they will never attempt to make us their obedient Colonists again.

Those smartly dressed Redcoats called my men the scum of the earth. They called them Dirty Shirts. Not anymore, they don't. Many can't because they are dead.

They outnumbered us 2-1, but with great vigilance, my ragtag band of Patriots with no training emerged victorious. We soundly defeated the most powerful military in the world, the boasted British Army of the Duke of Wellington. Not concerned with gentlemanly warfare, we used dirt, cotton bales, and sugar barrels to make an invincible barricade. This triumph is one for the history books. We conquered the conquerors of Europe. It's the best news since the Battle of Yorktown. Huzzah!

While our band played 'Yankee Doodle' and the Ursuline nuns prayed without ceasing, my mismatched misfits killed or wounded 2,500 of those 3,000 Lobsters within thirty minutes. Yes, a landslide in thirty minutes! I can only hope the Redcoat who slashed my hands and forehead when I was fourteen for refusing to clean the mud from his boots was among them.

They lost a full third of their army, but we are only down seven Americans. It was a spectacle of carnage and one of the most embarrassing defeats in British history. The ground was a sea of red, not from blood, but their obnoxious coats that covered almost every inch of the soil. The surviving scoundrels ran away through the swamp in a most shameful retreat. Good riddance.

Under my leadership, divided men from vastly different backgrounds came together and repelled a brutal invasion of our country. Using swords, cannon blasts, and rifle fire, I hail their undaunted courage. Natives of different states, acting together for the first time, reaped the fruits of an honorable union. I have never witnessed such dedication.

The British Commander, General Pakenham, believed my motley crew would wilt in his presence. Instead they killed him. First, they shot two horses from underneath him and then used their hunting rifles with expert precision to terminate him with a shot to the neck, as well as two other Generals, seven Colonels and seventy-

five other Officers. Not bad for some low-class Dirty Shirts, wouldn't you say?

My plan is to maintain martial law for several months in case those repulsive Brits dare to show their faces again. We will make sure they regret it if they do.

Thank you, Mr. President, for entrusting me with this tremendous responsibility.

Humbly in your service,
Major General Andrew Jackson

JEMMY GLOWS, EVEN MORE JUBILANT THAN ON OUR wedding day, and rushes over to embrace me. After a long bear hug, I finally break away. Then I sprint down the stairs, two steps at a time, holding my skirt high in a most unladylike fashion. It's a wonder I make it down the immense staircase without throwing out my knee.

"Huzzah! It's a miracle!" I shout, throwing open the door and losing all sense of decorum. "New Orleans has been saved! General Jackson and his mighty band of buccaneers have defeated the Brits and chased them out of Louisiana in disgrace!"

French John runs up from the cellar with a roar, his fists raised overhead. Once he catches sight of me, he bends over, roaring so hard that he can't speak. "Mrs. Madison, mon dieu!" he gasps, finally catching his breath. "What in the world are you wearing?"

I look down and burst into gales of laughter, too. Even embarrassing myself in front of Washington City can't dampen my happiness, not today. Needless to say, the wondrous news travels faster than lightning. Without further ado, Sukey helps me whisk off my farmhouse dress and slip into a gown befitting the occasion.

Then I throw open the Octagon doors for the jubilant

crowd gathered out front and ask the servants to light candles in all thirty-one windows. My goodness, I've never seen such overflowing rooms in all my years of entertaining. Even those who boycotted us after the burning of Washington City turn out, adding to the massive crowd.

By nighttime, there's no room to move. For hours, the servants stand outside holding flaming torches in the open windows. Thousands of joyous Americans fill the streets cheering, singing 'The Star-Spangled Banner,' and hoisting their own flaming torches. To my delight, our temporary home gains a new nickname, the House of One Thousand Candles.

Raucous celebrations continue for days with a constant deluge of fireworks, pealing bells, and bonfires galore. Spurred by our incredible victory, the Senate finally appropriates a whopping $500,000 to rebuild the President's House, the Capitol, and our other ruined Public Buildings. Huzzah, what an enormous sum! At last, it is settled. Washington City will serve as America's capital city into eternity. Full of his lost vigor, Jemmy pledges that reconstruction will begin right away.

CHAPTER 32
PEACE! PEACE!
FEBRUARY 1815

I love parties more than anyone in Washington City. However, after ten days of playing hostess, even I am relieved to resume the routines of daily life. In the late afternoon, French John and the servants shovel along New York Avenue in front of the Octagon, clearing away yet another deluge of snow. As usual, the beleaguered Jemmy locks himself away in his study where he's even quieter than usual. He's probably re-reading General Jackson's letter for the hundredth time. For once, I find myself alone and savor the rare tranquility after so many rowdy celebrations.

As I powder my face in my dressing room, loud knocking on the front door floats up the stairs, jarring me. I ignore it. After all, with the latest barrage of snow, no one of any importance would call on us today. Our unexpected visitor can return later. A heavenly silence prevails again for a moment, but then the pounding resumes with even more fervor. Some horses bray in the street, so I peek out the window and spy a handsome carriage. With a huff, I head downstairs to answer the door before our impatient caller breaks right through it.

Much to my shock, the Secretary to our American delegation in Belgium stands on our doorstep holding an ornate leather box. "Why, Mr. Hughes, what a surprise to find you standing out here in the cold!" I stammer.

"Well, hello, Mrs. Madison!" He gives a slight bow. "I certainly didn't expect you to answer the door."

"Please tell me what brings you here. I thought you were over in Ghent at the negotiations." I reach out to embrace him but then pull back and put a hand to my chest. "Oh, no! Did something go wrong over there?"

"Much the opposite, ma'am." He breaks into a wide smile. "We negotiated a fine treaty on Christmas Eve, ending the war once and for all! And Parliament has already ratified it."

"Good heavens, what wonderful news! But you're shivering out there, Mr. Hughes. I'm terribly sorry. Please do come in. Let me bring you to Mr. Madison right away." I scurry up the grand spiral staircase, ignoring my aching knee.

"Mrs. Madison, I do apologize for splattering snow on your lovely staircase," he says, following on my heels.

"I'll gladly trade a few icy puddles for peace." Indeed I am far too giddy to care. "Once you're finished, let me get you a big bowl of chicken and okra soup." I giggle at the prospect of the hostilities coming to an end, a dream come true.

By the time I reach the top of the stairs, I can't control myself a moment longer. "Jemmy, you won't believe this!" I bellow across the landing. "Mr. Hughes just arrived here from Ghent with a treaty in hand."

"Welcome home, Mr. Hughes," calls Jemmy as he rushes to greet him. "Thank you for your service to our country."

"Mr. President, it has been an honor. After years of negotiations, I finally bring you a real offer of peace, the Treaty of Ghent." Mr. Hughes opens the box and presses the document into my husband's trembling hands.

"Bravo! I've dreamt of this moment for so long. Come in,

come in, please." Jemmy beams as he shepherds us into his office.

"Edmund, please contact Secretary Monroe and the rest of the Cabinet," he calls to his personal secretary. "Have them report here right away."

We sit in a heavy silence as Jemmy reads through the entire document, line by line. I bite my lip so I don't pester him with the questions racing through my mind. Are the terms fair? Will this finally mean peace for us?

Eventually Jemmy looks up and releases a weary sigh. "Well, I'm far from thrilled." He throws the treaty onto his desk and rubs his brow as if to ward off a headache. "It just re-establishes the status quo all over again. We're right back where we started when the war began. It's little more than an end to the fighting and dying. But the biggest irony is that impressment isn't even mentioned. That was our main reason for declaring war in the first place."

His jaw tightens. "Of course, this makes the slaughter down in New Orleans totally unnecessary. We were already at peace but didn't know it yet."

Mr. Hughes stares at the floor, his face drained of color.

"Well, it did energize our national morale, Jemmy," I interject. "Maybe we don't gain anything in the treaty, but we don't lose anything either. Our new country just survived another war with the strongest power in the world."

"You're right, my dearest, as you always are." Jemmy sighs as a glow of contentment spreads across his face. "At last, we've come together as a nation, not just a group of individual states. We can rebuild our buildings, but we could never regain our lost honor."

"Hold your head up high, Mr. President." I beam at him. "Washington City may be in ashes, but we've earned the respect of the world."

News of the treaty spreads from one neighbor to the next

faster than a kitchen fire. By the time I return downstairs, a lively crowd has gathered in the street out front. As the Cabinet members scurry into the house, these citizens hope to witness the official proclamation of peace. The servants ring our dinner bell over and over again. Within minutes, other bells chime down the street. Soon joyous women stand on their doorsteps, banging on their pots and pans. Then the churches join in, pealing their bells nonstop. The ringing gains strength over Washington City, extending all the way to Georgetown. In my entire life, I will never enjoy a happier sound.

Overcome with jubilation, I throw open the front doors without informing the servants. Then I invite the swelling throngs into the drawing room and receive them in front of the stone fireplace. As our unexpected guests flood the entire downstairs, French John uncorks bottle after bottle of wine and offers a glass to everyone with a flourish, including the servants. Judging from his drunken escapades soon thereafter, our stately Master of Ceremonies makes sure to serve himself multiple times in rapid succession.

"It's peace! Peace!" I shout. This melodious word, now so unfamiliar on my tongue, springs from my lips in a never-ending refrain. Within seconds, our guests repeat it, too, with equal fervor. It's been absent from our vocabulary far too long. My heart is so full it may burst.

"If our envoys hadn't signed this weak treaty, our government wouldn't have been able to operate even six more months." Rosalie Calvert sniffs as she sips her champagne.

I am so elated that her pessimism doesn't irk me in the least.

A FEW DAYS LATER, THE REMAINING MEMBERS OF OUR delegation trickle back into town. Payne's trunks arrive as well, stuffed with his dapper new wardrobe. Much to my surprise, several crates of Russian and European artwork also appear on our doorstep. Apparently, he acquired these paintings on his travels. Alas, my beloved son himself never makes an appearance, so I can't ask him how he paid for these extravagent treasures.

John Quincy Adams informs me that Payne missed the delegation's ship in France and then again in England. Only another mother could understand my crushing disappointment, the sole damper on this wondrous occasion. I pray he is safe and will make his way home soon.

When Henry Clay returns to town, he calls on us right away. My face lights up as he smothers me in an affectionate hug. With a nervous smile, he shakes Jemmy's outstretched hand. "I'll be the first to say it's a darned bad treaty. Honest to God, it was the best we could do. The negotiations lasted almost as long as the war. You should've seen their first offer." He rolls his eyes. "It was outrageous. But the important thing is that we didn't lose any honor, territory, or rights."

"Agreed, and thank you for your heroic efforts," Jemmy responds. "We may not have won the war, but we won the peace. With Jackson's miracle in New Orleans, at least Americans feel victorious. That's what really matters—fortifying our national spirit."

"It is my honor, Mr. President. I do have a confession to make, though. I once believed you were too kind for the storms of war. Thankfully you have proven me quite wrong."

A few days later, the Senate ratifies the treaty with a rare unanimous vote. Copying the Octagon House's celebration after the victory in New Orleans, the citizens of Washington City put candles in every window, illuminating the capital in a flickering glow. The phenomenon of lights as beacons of peace spreads all over the country. In addition, schools and businesses close. Even legislatures across the country adjourn so everyone can participate in the boisterous celebrations.

Flanked by his Cabinet in his study, Jemmy signs the treaty into law. Shouts of "Peace! Peace!" echo throughout our crowded house.

With a grin, Paul grabs his violin and breaks into a rousing rendition of 'Madison's March.' When several guests bump into him, he jumps onto a chair and plays it over and over again.

Within a few hours, hundreds of demobilized soldiers march by the Octagon House, yelling three cheers in my honor. Jemmy and I stand on the steps and accept their salutes, bursting with pride.

"Bloody Brits!" Polly screeches in her harshest voice, perched on my shoulder. Needless to say, everyone breaks into fits of laughter. Such an honor I've never experienced, and God has blessed me with many more than I deserve.

I am elated. At first there was little enthusiasm for the war, but somehow, we rallied the nation. In addition, we won back our prestige, upholding the legacy of the first War of Independence. Finally, we developed our national identity with a sense of who we are and where we want to go. After all, how we perceive ourselves is even more important than how other countries view us. Now that America's national identity is secure, our potential on the world stage is unlimited.

Although a devout Federalist, former President Adams praises Jemmy's leadership, thrilling him to his core. "Despite a thousand faults and blunders, President Madison acquired more glory and established more union than Washington, Jefferson and Adams put together." At long last, we have united as one nation.

Jemmy issues a Thanksgiving Proclamation. My heart

soars along with his popularity, which surges overnight. No longer blamed for our national woes, he becomes a beloved hero. America embraces the Great Little Madison's dedication that I have cherished for so long. At long last, my fellow Americans now admire the man I admire most. We celebrate this small man with his small voice who has both a huge heart and a huge intellect.

"It's all thanks to you, my dear. I couldn't have done this without you, starting even before my election. You are truly my better half."

"And you are mine."

"Hail to the Presidentess!" squawks Polly, ruffling her feathers.

EPILOGUE - OUR LIFE AFTER THE WAR

Nothing could please me more than the satisfying conclusion of our Second War of Independence and Jemmy's miraculous redemption in the eyes of his countrymen and the world.

Much to our delight, the Federalist Party falls apart. With a nod to the tradition established by General Washington and followed by our dear friend, Mr. Jefferson, Jemmy refuses to run for a third term. Instead he ends his presidency on an extremely popular note, ushering in the Era of Good Feelings with the new President James Monroe, our fifth to hold the office. When we depart by steamboat after a month of farewell festivities, Jemmy is as giddy as a schoolboy on summer holidays, thrilled to leave the massive responsibilities of the office behind him. He never returns to Washington City.

We retire with our servants to Montpelier for twenty wonderful years. The stream of overnight guests is never-ending. Our new two-story ice house ensures a steady supply of my beloved iced creams. To everyone's amusement, I sometimes give Jemmy piggyback rides on our front porch.

Despite his lifetime of poor health, Jemmy outlives the other Founding Fathers. Presidents Adams and Jefferson both die within hours of each other on the same momentous day, July 4, 1826. Five years later in 1831, President Monroe also passes away on July 4. By 1836, Jemmy's valiant heart fails him. However, he refuses to prolong his life until July 4. Instead, my humble husband passes from this earth on June 28.

Words cannot capture the depth of my heartbreak. It tortures me to live without dear Jemmy by my side. To make matters even worse, I discover that my finances are in shambles. For years Jemmy paid off Payne's gambling debts. To spare me the anguish, he never informed me. As a result, I now face a mountain of bills with no means to pay them. To my horror, I find myself thrust back into the dire poverty of my youth.

Leaving Payne to manage my beloved Montpelier, I move back to Washington City with Sukey, Paul and Polly. Although I'm sure Payne tried his best, my debts only increase. Soon I must sell Montpelier.

My residence in Lafayette Square at 1520 H Street becomes known as the Little White House because a tradition develops. Before taking the oath of office, each president-elect calls on me and asks for my blessing. What an honor to call myself a friend to America's first twelve presidents. However, only Jemmy is my best friend, and he is the sole companion of my heart.

Aware of my impoverished state, Congress purchases Jemmy's official papers from me. However, they set up a trust to prevent Payne from accessing it. In all honesty, it's quite a relief. Try as he does, my precious son often falls under the spell of alcohol and spends beyond his means. When he goes to debtors' prison, it breaks my heart. If only I had the means to help him. How my poor boy suffers.

My nickname, Queen of Hearts, brings me such joy. Eventually I am the only living widow of our Founding Fathers, a relic of our country's heroic beginnings. In addition to a lifetime of free postage, I lay the first cornerstone of the Washington Monument, send the first telegram, and enjoy seeing my portrait featured on a silver dollar. I am truly blessed, far more than I deserve.

Despite my dire financial situation, I do host an annual open house on New Year's Day. It is just as crowded as the White House, as it is now called, which thrills me to no end. I can't afford to entertain otherwise, but I attend every party to which I am invited. Out of necessity, though, I must wear outdated dresses from my earlier days in Washington City. I even make a dress from the crimson red drapes that I saved from that dreadful fire back in 1814.

When I am 76, Congress gives me a permanent seat in the gallery, the first such distinction for a woman. The consent was unanimous, making it all the more meaningful. Let me assure you, I make frequent use of this priceless privilege. Their passionate debates still provide the best entertainment in Washington City. If I happen to arrive late, I request they begin anew, and they always oblige me.

❧

DOLLEY MADISON LEAVES THIS WORLD ON JULY 12, 1849, and her memorial services are the largest in American history. Calling her our "Queen Mother," President Zachary Taylor closes the Federal Government and orders a state funeral. In his eulogy, he declares her the "First Lady of the land for half a century," coining the term still in use today.

Should you catch a whiff of lilac while visiting Washington City, please think of Dolley.

DOLLEY MADISON'S FAVORITE RECIPES

MR. JEFFERSON'S SOFT GINGERBREAD
Molasses
Beef drippings (or lard)
Baking soda
Hot water
Flour
Ground ginger
Ground cinnamon
Powdered sugar

Mix 1 cup molasses (Dolley's "receipt" specified New Orleans molasses) with 2/3 cup fresh beef drippings. Add 1 1/4 teaspoons baking soda dissolved in 1/4 cup hot water. Sift your dry ingredients: 2 1/4 cups flour, 4 teaspoons ginger, and 1 tablespoon cinnamon. Next pour 3/4 cup hot water which has almost reached the boiling point into the molasses mixture alternately with the flour mixture. Beat thoroughly with a rotary or electric beater. The dough should be soft enough to pour. Bake in a shallow, well-greased baking dish in a preheated medium (350 degrees F.) oven 25 to 30 minutes, or until a toothpick inserted in the center of the cake comes out clean. Delicious served warm, sprinkled with powdered sugar.

---*The Presidents' Cookbook* (p. 90)

WOODBURY CINNAMON TEA CAKE
    Butter
    Sugar
    Flour
    Baking powder
    Cinnamon
    Milk

Cream 2 tablespoons butter with 1 cup sugar. Add 2 cups sifted flour mixed with 1 teaspoon baking powder and 2 tablespoons cinnamon. Add ½ cup milk and beat together thoroughly. Bake in a large pan in a medium (350 degrees F) oven for 30 minutes, or until done.

---*The Presidents' Cookbook* (p. 91)

DOLLEY MADISON'S LAYER CAKE
    Egg whites
    Butter
    Sugar
    Milk
    Cornstarch
    Flour
    Vanilla

Beat the whites of 8 eggs until stiff and in peaks. Put aside. Cream 1 cup butter with 2 1/2 cups sugar. Add 1 cup milk slowly, mixing well. Add 3/4 cup cornstarch and 3 cups sifted flour to the butter-egg mixture. Mix well and add 2 1/2 teaspoons vanilla. Fold in the egg whites carefully. Bake in 4 layer pans, well-greased, in a medium (350 degrees F.) oven for 30 to 35 minutes, or until the cake springs back when touched lightly. Cool on racks and frost with Dolley Madison's Caramel Sauce.

---*The Presidents' Cookbook* (p. 89)

༒

DOLLEY MADISON'S CARAMEL SAUCE

Brown sugar
Light cream
Butter
Vanilla

Mix well 3 cups brown sugar, 1 cup cream, and 2 tablespoons butter. Put mixture in the top of a double boiled and cook gently for 20 minutes. Just before removing from the stove, after the caramel has thickened, add 1 teaspoon vanilla, stir constantly. Remove and cool. Fill the layers of the cake and put icing on top as well.

---*The Presidents' Cookbook* (p. 89)

AUTHOR'S NOTE

The vast majority of the historical events described in this book actually took place, including Dolley's infamous 'squeezes' held at the President's House. Most of the dialogue as well as Dolley's thoughts are conjecture, based on my extensive research into Dolley and James Madison as well as the other important figures of that time period. However, some direct quotes are included as well.

My museum research included visits to Montpelier, the James Madison Museum of Orange County Heritage, the U.S. Capitol, the White House, the Octagon House Museum, the National Museum of the U.S. Navy, Dumbarton House, Riversdale House Museum, Fort Washington National Park, Bladensburg Waterfront Park, Star-Spangled Banner Flag House, Fort McHenry National Monument and Historic Shrine, Maryland Historical Society, USS Constitution Museum, and the National Society U.S. Daughters of 1812 Library and Museum.

Please refer to the Selected Bibliography for the significant sources of my research.

SELECTED BIBLIOGRAPHY

CHILDREN'S BOOKS

Fritz, Jean, *The Great Little Madison*, New York: Paperstar, 1989.

Kent, Zachary, *Dolley Madison*, Berkeley Heights, NJ: Winslow Publisher, 2010.

Krensky, Stephen, *Sisters of Scituate Light*, New York: Dutton Children's Books, 2008.

Krull, Katherine, *Women Who Broke the Rules: Dolley Madison*, New York: Bloomsbury, 2015.

Redding, Anna Crowley, *Rescuing the Declaration of Independence*, New York: Harper, 2020.

ADULT BOOKS

Alden, Robert Ames, *Flight of the Madisons,* Fairfax County Council of the Arts, 1974.

Allgor, Catherine, *Parlor Politics*, Charlottesville: University of Virginia Press, 2000.

Berkin, Carol, *Wondrous Beauty*, New York: Alfred A. Knopf, 2014.

Borneman, Walter B., *1812*, New York: Harper Perennial, 2005.

Callcott, Margaret Law, *Mistress of Riversdale*, Baltimore: The Johns Hopkins University Press, 1991.

Cheney, Lynn, *James Madison,* New York: Viking, 2014.

Feldman, Noah, *The Three Lives of James Madison*, New York: Picador, 2017.

Groom, Winston, *Patriotic Fire*, New York: Vintage Books, 2006.

Hickey, Donald R., *The War of 1812*, Chicago: University of Illinois Press, 1995.

Jennings, Paul, *A Slave in the White House*, Chicago: University of Chicago, 1865.

Muller, Charles G., *The Darkest Day: 1814*, Philadelphia: J.B. Lippincott Company, 1963.

Ozer, Mark N., *Washington DC and the War of 1812*, Mark N. Ozer, 2013.

Pitch, Anthony S., *The Burning of Washington*, Annapolis, MD: Naval institute Press, 2000.

Webb, Heather, *Becoming Josephine*, New York: Plume, 2014.

ACKNOWLEDGMENTS

Huzzah! It has been an incredible honor to tell the story of America's *first* First Lady, Dolley Madison, and her crucial role during the forgotten War of 1812. So much more than a wonderful hostess, she was President Madison's most valuable advisor and a skilled politician in her own right.

Thank you, Queen Dolley, for your bravery as well as your valiant efforts to unite our country during such divisive and terrifying times. We are forever indebted to you for establishing so many beloved national traditions and creating a sense of "Americanness" that has endured to this day.

My heart is filled with gratitude for those who supported me writing this book, helping to make my dream into a reality. A big thank you to all my friends, cheerleaders, and fellow history geeks who routinely asked, "How's Dolley coming along?" Your encouragement truly kept me going.

A special thank you to my dear friend, Jayda Justus. Several years ago, she suggested we attend a lecture on Dolley Madison by Montpelier's CEO at the Virginia Museum of History and Culture in Richmond. That talk inspired this novel! Thank you, Jayda, for your unwavering support as I retraced Dolley's fashionable footsteps.

I must also gush about my outstanding writing partner and wonderful friend, Ann Tierney Prochnow, who read at least five (more like ten) versions of every chapter without once complaining. Thank you, Ann, from the bottom of my heart! Hoya Saxa!

Karen Chase, thank you for your loving support and wise counsel all along the route. I couldn't do it without you, Felix, and it wouldn't be nearly as fun.

Thank you to those who took the time to read and write such thoughtful blurbs—Jenny Cote, Kathryn Tone, Jayda Justus, Karen Chase, Judith Kalaora, Steven Smith, Susan Rowe, Annette Benbow, Joanne Stanley, Donna Wilson, and Mary Patterson of the Little Bookshop.

Heartfelt thanks to my early readers—Mary Helen Sheriff, Grace Sammon, Bernie and Sam McNamee, Martha Tutrani, Mary O'Connor, Alice DeVriendt, Katie Sullivan and her friend Alice.

To my amazing fellow "tour guides" on Bookish Road Trip via Facebook—Mary Sheriff, Julie Valerie, Melissa Face, Grace Sammon, Josie Brown and Meredith Stoddard. Thank you for always being just a text away with excellent advice and a reason to laugh. Come get lost with us! And Julie, thanks a ton for the graphics! BAM!

A huge shout-out to Dane at Ebook Launch for another fabulous cover! Bravo! And many thanks to Sheena Billet and Alison Jack for their wonderful editing services.

A big thank to the dedicated museum professionals for their hospitality and generosity with their time and resources: Hilary Hicks at the Montpelier Foundation; Bethany Sullivan at the James Madison Museum of Orange County Heritage; Ann Wass at the Riversdale House Museum; Scott Scholz at the Dumbarton House; and Patti Maclay, President of the

District of Columbia Society, National Society U.S. Daughters of 1812.

To my fabulous interpreter friends—Judith Kalaora who portrays Dolley; Kyle Jenks as James Madison; and Charmaine Crowell-White as Sukey. I have learned so much from each of you!

To Chuck Schwam, Alan Hoffman and my fellow American Friends of Lafayette, HUZZAH! Thank you for your love, support, and fun-filled excursions. Vive Lafayette! To Jenny Cote, I raise all eight spoons to you! Julien, I hope you find this a cozy read.

A heartfelt thanks to Bernie and Sam who suffered through the many ups-and-downs of writing this book (i.e. lots of drama), always encouraging me along the way. Last but not least, a big belly rub for my furry feline assistant, Zeke, who slept through the War of 1812, snoring at my feet.

ABOUT THE AUTHOR

Libby McNamee is an author, public speaker, and lawyer. She loves to learn about America's history and explore its historical sites. Dolley Madison and the War of 1812 was named "Best Book in U.S. Historical Fiction," by Pinnacle Book Achievement Awards in Fall 2021. Her first published novel, Susanna's Midnight Ride: The Girl Who Won the Revolutionary War, was named #1 in Juvenile Fiction by the 2020 Independent Publisher Book "IPPY" Awards and the 2020 Pinnacle Book Awards. In addition, it was a Finalist in the 2020 Best Book Awards for Historical Fiction and the 2019 Young Adult Virginia Author "YAVA" Award.

A native of Boston, she graduated from Georgetown University and Catholic University School of Law. She also served as a U.S. Army JAG Officer in Korea, Bosnia, Germany, and Washington State. Libby lives in Richmond, Virginia, with her patient husband, history-guru son, and zany cat.

Please join Libby's Dispatch email newsletter at LibbyMcNamee.com for historical tidbits every month. She would love to talk to your school, historical society, and book club in person or by zoom! Huzzah!

A BIG FAVOR

Dear Reader,

Thank you so much for taking the time to read *Dolley Madison and the War of 1812*. It means the world to me—and Dolley.

Would you please do me a big favor and review this book on Amazon and Goodreads? It doesn't have to be long or fancy. In fact, something short that comes from the heart would be perfect! Reviews are so important for authors, especially independent ones like me.

Also, the next time you go to your library, would you please ask them to carry this book?

I am so grateful for your help.

Cheers!

Libby McNamee

LIBBY MCNAMEE'S FIRST NOVEL "SUSANNA'S MIDNIGHT RIDE"

THE GIRL WHO WON THE REVOLUTIONARY WAR

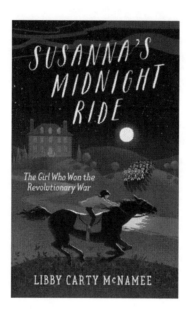

* Winner—Juvenile Fiction by 2020 Independent Publisher ("IPPY") Book Awards

* Winner—Juvenile Fiction by 2020 Pinnacle Book Awards

* Finalist—Historical Fiction by 2020 Best Book Awards

* Finalist—2019 Young Adult Virginia Author "YAVA" Award

Made in the USA
Middletown, DE
30 May 2023

31518902R00154